Life Beneath
the Willow

J.C. Hamm

Life Beneath the Willow
A Novel By J.C. Hamm

A Davenport Writes, LLC Publication/July 2016

This is a work of fiction. All names, characters, and incidents are the product of the author's imagination. Any resemblance to real person, living or dead, is entirely coincidental.

Published by
Davenport Writes, LLC

Printed in the United States of America

To Lydia

In Loving Memory of
Our German Shepherd,
Sophia
2003-2014

J.C. HAMM

Acknowledgements

I first and foremost I want to Thank God for the many talents He has given me and for every breath I take. For everything He has done for me and the blessing of the family and friends He has given me.

Thank You to my Family my and Friends, to my husband Matt, and our two boys, my parents, my sisters and my niece and nephews for their unconditional love, support and patience for all that I do. Thank you to my family of Authors for their ongoing support and networking. Thank Larry Stumbo, Matthew Davenport, Jordyn Meryl, Sue Raymond, LaVina Vanorny Barcus and the rest of the team at Davenport Writes.

Thank You to my Editor Courtney Bebensee.

Thank you to Gary and Jan Ash, Kelsey Stubbe, and Tim Bartleman.

Thank You to Adam Meirick and Lydia Polzin for modeling for the cover.

Thank You Katy Jo Kimbley for the cover design.

A Special Thank You To All of Our Service Men and Women who have served and are still serving our country.

CHAPTER 1

Will ran quickly through the trees. He jumped over rocks, logs and wooded debris, as he followed the sound of her piercing screams. His heart raced wildly as he vigorously changed directions through another brush of overgrown weeds. The thick thorny bushes snagged his bare forearms and the sting of the razor thin cuts made him swing his arms wildly to shield his face as he ran through and under the branches.

He slid to the ground, stopping himself at the edge of a steep cliff just beyond the tree line.

He wheezed as he tried to collect his breath. His body numb, his muscles pulsed with every heartbeat and the bloody cuts on his arms stung. And for a moment, there was silence. Her screams had stopped. There was no breeze rustling through the leaves. There were no birds chirping in the trees -nothing but silence.

He took a deeply needed breath as he stared across the deep cliff. A beautiful young willow tree sat on the edge of the other side. It's soft flowing branches swayed slightly as if it was waving to him. A warm glow appeared from behind the tree's trunk, illuminating the shiny leaves into a rainbow of colors. The tree turned quickly from green to yellow then orange. The leaves then began to wilt and fizzle as they turned red, and into what looked like millions of individual tiny flames. In an instant, they burst into wisps of grey smoke, leaving the thin branches hanging cold and alone. A chill ran up his spine and throughout his body. The hairs on the back of his neck stood upright, as the tree turned glossy and transparent. His heart rate elevated as the glass like tree shattered as she screamed.

"DADDY!!!"

He leaped back to his feet and sprinted up the steep incline toward the sound of his daughter's painful screams. At the top, he tried to catch his breath as he searched frantically in circles, desperately trying to find her location. His panic escalated as confusion set in on which direction he should go. Her screams became louder and seemed to surround him.

Heart pounding, he instantly climbed an old oak tree. The rough branches scratched his palms as he climbed higher and higher. He slipped as a limb snapped beneath his weight and he fell like a heavy rag doll. His eyes grew wide as his body lie broken and shattered on the ground. He screamed her name with his final breath.

Honor sat on the edge of her father's bed. She shook him gently by the shoulders.

"Dad," she spoke softly, trying not to startle him.

Will snapped out of his dream and instantly wrapped his arms around her in relief. She hugged him back, resting her head against his sweaty t-shirt. She could hear his heart pounding.

"Are you alright?" she asked pulling away from his chest. She watched as sweat dripped from the tips of his shoulder length hair.

"Yeah," he answered, his voice dry from exertion. "Yeah, I'm fine," he assured her as he brushed back her black curly hair and he kissed her mocha-toned forehead.

She watched him as he paused to collect his thoughts. It was rare to see him so vulnerable, as he always was after one of his nightmares. The dazed look in his eyes as he regained his sense of reality.

"You were screaming in your sleep again. Do you want to talk about it?" she asked, interrupting his silent blank stare.

"No. I'm okay," he assured her with a quick smile.

He has had these dreams before and never has he ever told her about a single one. She knew her father well. They had no other secrets from each other. But his nightmares were his own and he kept them to himself. But it never stopped her from asking.

She smiled back at him as she stood up by his bedside. "I'll get the coffee started."

He nodded at her as he dropped his feet from the bed to the floor. He sat up straight as he adjusted his wet shirt.

"You may want to take a shower," she teased him.

"I'll do that," he answered, staring at the floor and paying no attention to her taunt.

"Good, cause you stink," she teased him again, this time catching his attention. He grabbed one of his pillows and threw it at her as she darted for the door; she reached the hallway as the pillow hit the wall next to the door.

She poked her head around the doorframe. "Your aim is off," she taunted him.

"Get out of here!" He grinned, as he threw another pillow at her.

2

~ ~ ~

Finn, their German shepherd, leaped up from his doggie bed to greet Honor as she entered the kitchen.

"Morning Finn." She knelt down as she welcomed the dog into her arms and petted him. She walked over to the kitchen counter to the coffee maker and measured the coffee grounds into the filter basket. She then poured water into the water compartment. She flipped the switch on and waited for the gurgling sound of the water moving.

She grabbed Finn's leash hanging from the small hook along side the door.

"Come on boy," She latched the leash to Finn's collar and led him out the door of their apartment.

The apartment building was a large, three-story house that had been converted into seven small units. Honor and her father's apartment was on the first floor and was one of the smaller units which was perfect for the two of them. They didn't have much, just the necessary items. Honor's room was the larger of the two but only contained a bed, a dresser, a nightstand and a large bookshelf filled with books. She never really favored having toys or knick-knacks. Her love was books. Will had only a bed, a dresser and a large footlocker at the end of his bed.

The neighborhood settled just outside the downtown area of Des Moines, was filled with large, three-story houses similarly used as apartments buildings.

Honor walked Finn quickly around the block as she always did every morning before school. The spring air smelled of fresh rain that had fallen the night before. Finn stopped at his usual spots to sniff out and remark his territory.

~ ~ ~

Will had showered and was dressed. He was sitting at the kitchen table with his coffee and two bowls of oatmeal when she returned home.

"Hungry?" he asked her.

She unhooked Finn's collar from the leash, placing the leash back on its hook by the door.

"Yes," she answered, as she sat down at the table across from him.

Will held out his hands to her. She placed her hands into his and they bowed their heads.

"Heavenly Father, thank you for all you have given us and the many blessings we don't always see. Thank you for this food that we are about to receive. Please bless it to fill and nourish our bodies. Keep, guide and protect us. In your Name, Amen." He gently squeezed her hands and then released them as he smiled and winked at her.

Honor stirred her hot cereal and she looked up at her father. He was reading the newspaper eating his oatmeal.

"Dad?"

"Yes?" he acknowledged her from behind the paper.

"How come you don't ever tell me about them?" she asked him as she blew on her hot cereal before taking a bite.

"About who, sweetheart?"

"Your nightmares," she inquired quietly.

"Did you get your homework done?" he asked her.

"Don't elude the question," she responded quickly, annoyed that he was ignoring her question.

"Elude?" he looked at her, surprised by her choice of words.

"Yes elude, evade, circumvent, avoid the answering of my question."

"Have you been reading the dictionary again?" he asked, hiding back behind his paper.

Honor stared at him as she ate another spoonful of oatmeal. "Dad!" she repeated with her mouth full.

"Did you get your homework done?" he asked again from behind his paper.

"What?"

"Homework. Assignments given to students to do outside of the classroom. Is it done?"

"Yes, it's done," she answered him as she continued to stare at him. "Dad?"

Will looked around the newspaper at her.

"Baby, you know I don't like telling you about those things."

"I know. It's just that I've never heard you scream that loud before. And you said my name in your sleep. I just thought it was different than all the others."

Will put down his paper and looked his daughter in the eyes. "I'm sorry if I scared you."

"Was it about your tours?"

"Yeah it's always about the tours," he assured her as he looked at the clock on the kitchen wall. "Finish up, we're going to be late."

Honor ate her last big spoonful of oatmeal as she jumped up from the table. She gathered her father's cereal bowl along with her own and rinsed them off in the kitchen sink. Finn waited patiently next to his food and water dish, as she scooped out his daily serving of food and replenished his water.

Will walked to his bedroom and opened the drawer to his nightstand. He pulled out his pistol, a Colt 1911. He double checked the safety and glided it into his concealed holster inside his pants and straightened his shirt over his waistline as he walked out of the room.

Honor was waiting next to the door with her nose in a book.

"Ready?" He asked. She nodded as she grabbed her school bag and they walked out the door together.

~~~

Will dropped Honor off at middle school then headed to work. He arrived at the housing development where the framing company he worked for was finishing one of the houses. He had worked for the company for about a year and was very pleased with the work and the skills he had learned in such a short time.

He put on his black ball cap, which had the Marine Corps emblem embroidered on it. Looking in his rear view mirror he tucked his hair back behind his ears and straighten the hat. As he got out of his truck, he flipped back the floor mat beneath the steering wheel, uncovering the concealed safety box built-in beneath his seat. He unlocked the box and placed his pistol inside. He locked the box and replaced the floor mat then closed the door to his truck.

He walked around to the other side of his truck and reached into his toolbox. He grabbed his tool belt and put it on around his waist. He then pulled out his nail gun and a hose from the box.

He acknowledged the other men on the crew with a nod as he walked over to the compressor and plugged in his hose and nail gun.

"Will!" Richard called out to him from behind.

Will turned around. "Yes sir," He responded politely toward the owner of the company.

"I wanted to talk to you for a minute."

"Sure, what can I do for you, sir?"

"First, I just wanted you to know what a great job you are doing. You are here on time every day and I can always count on you to make the deadlines on time."

"Thank you, Sir. I appreciate that."

"Which makes it hard for me to let you go."

"Excuse me, I don't understand?" Will felt defensive.

"Will, I'm being forced to make some cuts. After this development, I can only run two, four men crews and with the other guys being here longer than you, as much as I regret it, I'm going to have to let you go."

"Sir, you don't understand. I have a daughter to take care of. This job is all we have to keep us afloat," Will pleaded. "I need this job."

"I know and I am sorry," Richard handed him an envelope. "Here's your check. It includes your paid time off you never took and I added a little extra for the inconvenience. And like I said, I'm sorry. If things change in the future, you'll be the first one I call."

Will took the envelope and stared at it for a moment. He felt the veins in his arms burn and his anxiety grow. He took a deep breath, and held it for a moment as he pushed back the thoughts in his head he so desperately wanted to release onto his boss.

"Thank you, Sir," he replied as politely as he could. He released his breath slowly as he turned around back to the compressor before his anger could turn against him.

He unplugged his hose and nail gun, then walked back to his truck. Richard watched as Will loaded his tools back into his toolbox.

~~~

Will held in his feelings the best he could as he made his way to the bank. He deposited his check in the drive-thru ATM so he could avoid conversations with the bank teller and other people. He then drove home, parking his truck on the street outside his apartment.

He turned off the ignition; his face grew warm as he threw his hat from his head onto the dashboard. He then grasped the steering wheel as tight as he could. His knuckles began to turn white from the pressure as he squeezed the wheel. He wanted to punch something, the window, the steering wheel, his boss, anything. He focused on keeping himself in control. He closed his eyes as he inhaled for four seconds then exhaled for four seconds to slow down his breathing. He gave out a deep gasp as tears of anger and fear enveloped him. He tried to fight back his tears but they streamed down his cheeks. His body tightened as he began to think that all the hard work from the past year was now gone. The promise of a good life now broken to the uncertainty that loomed. How was he to budget his last paycheck, the only money he had until he could find a new job, and for what? To just to start over at the bottom and work his way back up.

The rent was already behind and his only savings were invested in the toolbox in the back of his truck.

He wiped his face on his sleeve as he sniffled back self-pity and took in a deeply needed breath.

"Okay. Okay, Lord, what's next?" he said aloud. He closed his eyes and prayed silently for the Lord to take what happened this morning and make it into a new opportunity. As he prayed, his thoughts cleared as his face cooled and he felt his body relax. His quietness in prayer has always helped him cope. This was Will's peace, his assurance that he will get through whatever life throws at him. This is how he dealt with his tours in Iraq, the loss of his wife, the trials of raising their daughter on his own and this is how he will deal with his new financial setback.

He took another deep breath as he opened his eyes. Now calm, he got out of his truck and retrieved his pistol from the lock box, placing it in his holster and straightening his shirt as he walked into the apartment building.

Finn rushed to the door to greet Will as he opened the door.

"Hey boy. Looks like you get me for the day."

Will opened the refrigerator and grabbed one of his bottles of beer. As he closed the door he noticed the picture of Honor that hung eye level on the door of the freezer. He sighed and placed the bottle back into the fridge.

He made a fresh pot of coffee. He sat down at the table with his tablet, and began his search for a new job.

After a few hours of making some calls on a few ads and sending out his resume to several local job services, he decided to prioritize his bills.

He shuffled through his stack of bills and started to realize the financial hole he was facing. Utilities and the rent were due. He was already behind on his four credit cards that were maxed to their limits. He had been paying the minimum payments about every other month. He dreaded the calls he knew he would start getting soon. He worried, not knowing where his next paycheck would come from, let alone finding ways to feed himself and his daughter. He had been living paycheck to paycheck for so long he hadn't enough money to set aside for savings.

Will picked up his cell phone and scrolled through his contact list to his mother's number. He hesitated for a moment before hitting send. He let it ring twice before he changed his mind and hit the end button.

He stared at his phone. "Lord, what am I doing?"

His phone rang. It was his mother.

"Mom," he answered.

"William, honey, it's good to hear your voice. I notice that I had a missed call. Did you try to call me?" She spoke loudly over the phone.

"Yeah, I did. How are you?" Holding the phone away from his ear.

"Oh you know same old, same old. How about you? How's Honor?"

"She's good, we are both good."

"Is she there? I'd like to talk to her."

"She's still in school Mom."

"Yeah I suppose she would be. Shouldn't you be working or did you finally take a day off?"

"Ah that's kinda why I called you. They had to let me go."

"Oh Honey I'm sorry, what happened?"

"The builder just had to cut back for awhile. And since I was the last one hired I was their first pick for layoff. I'm looking for another job right now, but I'm a little short," he took a deep breath. "I was wondering if maybe you could lend me some money. I'll pay you back."

"I know you will. How much do you need?"

"Ah I don't know, three thousand? Just to get some of the bills caught up."

"No problem, how soon do you need it?"

"Soon, if you can send it?"

"Tell you what, why don't you and Honor come down this weekend and I'll write you a check for whatever you need. It would be good to see you two and catch up."

"I don't know mom, I really need to set up some interviews this weekend and...."

"William," she interrupted him. "If you need the money, I need to see my granddaughter. So just come for the weekend."

"Mom, you know I can't."

"There is a difference between can't and won't. You and I both know that you can. You just have to want to."

"Mom."

"Don't Mom me. It's been a long time since you have been home and I think you are able to handle a few days of visiting your mother."

"I'll see what I can do," Will responded quietly.

"Perfect, I'll be expecting you."

"Mom I didn't say - " He tried to argue.

"I'm not taking 'No' for answer, William," she interrupted him again. "I'll see you this weekend."

"Fine," he gave in. "Maybe just for the day on Saturday."

"Good. Oh William, honey, I got someone calling me on the other line. I love you and I'll see you soon. Bye," she said as she hung up on him before giving him a chance to say another word.

Will took a deep breath. Finn came over to him and rested his chin on Will's lap.

"Well, looks like we are going on a road trip boy."

~~~

Honor paid no attention to the three girls whispering and giggling behind her, as she read a book like she always did every day at school during lunch. She never really made friends with the other girls in her class. Most of them consider her to be strange or weird. She always had her nose in a book and the only time she actually interacted with others was during physical education, where she let her competitive side run wild. The boys her age only talked to her because they wanted to get her on their team, knowing that she was one of the stronger girls and could help them win the games they played.

This attention from some of the popular boys drove the popular girls, like the three sitting behind her, mad with envy. Amber Harrington and her two friends, Madison and Taylor, treated Honor cruelly at times, poking fun at the way she dressed, usually in her jeans and t-shirt and Converse. They'd also pick on her about her unusual name. They come up with nicknames like 'on her' or sometimes call her Connor because she dressed like a tomboy.

She suddenly felt something land in her hair. She brushed her fingers through her thick black hair to find a wad of bubble gum. She examined the sticky wad carefully, as the girls continued to giggle loudly behind her.

Disgusted, she removed it easily from the few strands of hair it was stuck on. Calmly she stood up from her chair and walked over to the girls. She tossed the wad of gum on Amber's lunch tray.

"You dropped this," she said calmly, then turned away, walking back to her seat.

"No I didn't. I threw it in the trash," Amber implied loudly.

Honor stopped. She took a deep breath, she felt her face warm from the embarrassment as other students looked at her, a few of them pointing and giggling from Amber's remark. Honor turned back around and walked quickly back to the girl's table.

"What are you looking at, Connor?" Amber asked in a snobby tone.

Honor grabbed Amber's tray and flung it into her lap. The lunchroom became quiet as the other students continued to watch the commotion between the girls.

"Ah, what the hell." Amber jumped up in shock, her clothes covered with the lunchroom special.

Amber's face turned red as the other kids were now laughing and pointing at her. "You're gonna pay for this," she threatened as she lunged at Honor, grabbing the back of her shirt, and swinging her around. The students stood to their feet and started to chant, "Fight! Fight! Fight!" Pumping their fists in the air.

Honor quickly defended herself as Amber attempted to punch her. She blocked Amber's punch, grabbed her wrist and swung it around her back. She then kicked Amber's feet out from under her and glided her face down to the floor, pinning her on the floor with her knee on her back and her wrist locked against her back. Her father had showed her this move and she smiled in amazement that it actually worked.

"Let go of me you freak!" Amber winced as she struggled on the floor.

Honor felt someone from behind her touch her shoulders. "That will be enough, McFadden."

Honor looked up. Mr. Sanders, the principal, stood behind her with an unpleasant look on his face. Honor quickly released Amber.

Mr. Sanders helped Amber to her feet. She rubbed her arm and glared at Honor. The other students settled down as Mr. Sanders looked around the room at them; then turned back to the two girls.

"I hope you punish her. She nearly broke my arm," Amber whimpered.

"Come on, my office now," Mr. Sanders said sternly.

"And she ruined my new shirt," she continued to complain.

"That's enough Amber. We can talk about it in my office along with your parents," he tried to guide them both to the hall.

"But I didn't do anything," Amber pleaded.

"In my office now!" He gave his final warning.

Both girls gathered their things from their tables; then walked quietly out of the lunchroom. Mr. Sanders walked behind them as they made their way to the office.

"Amber, go to the nurse and have her look at your arm," he instructed her. "Then meet me back here in my office."

Amber walked into the nurse's office. She was still whimpering about her arm as Honor sat down in the chair next to the principal's door and pulled her book out.

"Janis, could you get me the contact information for the parents of Amber Harrington and Honor McFadden, please?" He asked the secretary.

"Yes sir," she replied.

Janis started typing on the computer and wrote down the information on a piece of paper. She stepped away from her desk and walked into Mr. Sander's office handing him the paper. On her way out she noticed the book Honor was reading.

"Voids? That sounds like an interesting book. What is it about?" Janis asked.

"It's about two geologists investigating earthquakes, only to find out that they are not caused naturally but by empty spaces in the ground where oil was extracted."

"Wow, who wrote it?"

"LaVina Vanorny-Barcus."

"I'll have to look that one up," she smiled as she sat down at her and continued with her work.

Amber came out from the nurse's office with a bag of ice on her wrist. She rolled her eyes at Honor as she sat down in a chair across from her. Honor avoided eye contact and stuck her nose back in her book.

~~~

It wasn't long before Will arrived at the school. The principal had a short meeting with Honor and her father. Mr. Sanders then asked Honor to go back in the other room so he could talk with her father alone.

Honor sat down with her book. She could feel the glares through the pages and tried her best not to look up from behind her shield, as Amber continued to stare at her from across the room. Amber's mother had arrived and was sitting next to Amber as they waited for their turn to talk to the principal.

Amber's mother sat cross-legged with her top leg bouncing impatiently and her arms crossed against her chest. She was dressed like a casual business women: a slightly too short black skirt and a blouse with a low V-neck, that was barely covered by a petite, pale pink blazer. She, too, had been staring at Honor. Will opened the Principal's office door and walked into the room. Amber's mother quickly changed her body language as she straightened her blouse and skirt. Will paid no attention to the women as she batted her eyes at him, smiling nervously hoping for him to glance at her. Honor rolled her eyes at Amber and her mother as she stood up. She was annoyed at the thought that women like Amber's mother were drooling over her father.

"Come on, get your stuff," he said as he opened the door to the hallway. Honor grabbed her bag and followed him.

Will remained silent as he walked across the street to where he had parked his truck. Honor paced herself behind him nervously. She had never been in this much trouble before. She knew by the way her father walked quickly to the truck ahead of her, that he was upset. He pulled his keys from his pocket and unlocked the doors with the remote.

"So what did he say?" Honor asked cautiously as she got into the truck.

"Two weeks-you're suspended for two weeks," he answered as he started the engine. "What were you thinking?" He asked in firm tone as he drove down the street.

Honor shrugged her shoulders.

"How could you possibly think that what you did would resolve the situation?"

"I don't know, I guess I just lost control."

"Honor, you nearly broke her wrist," he raised his voice.

"What was I supposed to do? She was about to hit me," she snapped back. "I just did what you showed me to do to defend myself."

"I showed you that, thinking you would use it only in extreme cases."

"Yeah, she was attacking me so I stopped her and it worked."

"Of course it worked, she's like eighty pounds of blond hair. But you still didn't have to use so much force."

"Okay, I'm sorry."

"Well, you're going to be. You're grounded for those two weeks plus all the chores I can think of during that time."

"What? That's not fair," she whined.

"What's not fair is, you starting a fight and getting to stay home from school for two weeks."

"I didn't start it."

"So the lunch tray just jumped off the table? You could have walked away," he snapped at her.

"I tried but she... she." Honor bit her lip and looked down at the floorboards of the truck. Her eyes started to water.

"She what?" he asked her, staring at the road ahead of them.

"Never mind," she sniffled as she turned her face toward her window so he wouldn't see her cry.

Will stopped the truck and turned to her. "Hey, I'm sorry. I didn't mean to snap at you that way. Don't cry, please, I'm sorry."

"It's not you." Honor wiped her face on the collar of her shirt. "I'm just sick of Amber and all the other girls. I just couldn't take it anymore," she sobbed, "and you always told me not to be afraid to stick up for myself."

"I know, I did say that," Will said as he looked at her for a moment. He realized he couldn't be upset with her for sticking up for herself. That was the way he raised her. He took a deep breath.

"There are times when conflicts should be handled by force and other times peacefully. In your case, maybe you should have talked with a teacher right away instead of throwing her lunch at her."

Honor smiled a little as she remembered the look on Amber's face when she had done that.

"It's not funny," he said sternly but with a smile. "I thought you and that girl were friends?"

"That was two years ago."

"So, what happened?"

"She got boobs and started wearing make-up. Then she told me that I wasn't pretty enough to be her friend anymore."

"Well, I guess she really doesn't know what pretty is. You're the most beautiful girl I know," he said nudging her, making her smile.

"Sorry you had to leave work to come get me."

"That's okay. I wasn't doing much work anyway."

~~~

Jerry their landlord was walking out of the apartment building as Will and Honor arrived home. Will had been avoiding him since the beginning of the month knowing he didn't have enough for rent.

"Hey, why don't you go and get Finn. I'm sure he needs to be walked," Will asked her as he tucked his pistol back into his holster from the lock box.

"Okay," she said as she jumped out of the truck and ran ahead of her father. She smiled at Jerry as she passed him.

"Will, I'm glad I caught you," Jerry greeted him.

"Ah, yeah, me too. Look Jerry, I will have the money at the beginning of next week." Will watched his daughter enter the building, making sure she wasn't listening.

"No can do, Will. I've got people ready to look this weekend. I told you three months ago that I've got to have the rent on time."

"I know and I'm sorry, but I just had a setback, and I'm going to have the money first thing Sunday morning for you I promise," he pleaded with him.

"I want it Friday morning and no later. If you don't have it by then I'm going to have to ask you to be out by the weekend," Jerry started to walk away.

Will stopped him.

"Please, Jerry, can you just give me the weekend? I'll have the money plus the next month's rent. If I just have the weekend to get it. Please, just give me a chance."

"Will, I'm sorry. I can't give you any more extensions. Look, if I gave everyone as many chances as I've given you, my bills wouldn't get paid. Now I need it by Friday or you're going to have to find somewhere else to live."

"Yeah, okay." Will turned back toward the house. Honor was on her way out the door with Finn.

"Everything okay?" she asked, noticing that he was upset.

"Yeah, everything good with you?" He faked a smile.

"Yep. You want to walk with us? Or do you have to go back to work?"

"I'd much rather go for a walk with you," Will put his arm around her shoulder and kissed the top of her head.

~~~

"Come and get it," Will called Honor to the kitchen.

Honor sat down at the table. Will brought the pot over to the table and took the lid off.

"Wal-la!" he announced proudly.

Honor looked in the pot. "Mac 'n' cheese, again?"

"What, you love Mac 'n' cheese!"

"I loved it on Saturday and I didn't mind having it on Sunday. But dad, really, three times in a row?"

"What? I changed it up. Look I put hot dogs in it," he said proudly.

Honor looked at her father. She knew he wasn't much of a cook but she expected a little more.

"Look, I know this is not your ideal dinner. Especially three nights in a row, but it's what we've got. And we've..."

"We've got to make the most of what we've got," she said with him in unison. "Okay, I'm sorry, it looks great. Thank you."

"Thank you. Let's pray." He smiled as he sat down and bowed his head.

"Heavenly Father, thank you for this day and the gifts you have given us. Lord please give us the guidance we need in the decisions we make and patience in our time of need. Help me find a job that will fit our needs and serve you Lord. Thank you for this meal we are about to eat. May it fill and nourish our bodies. Keep, guide and protect us. In your name. Amen."

"Amen," Honor repeated quietly as she looked at him with concern.

Will started to portion out the Mac 'n' cheese when he noticed that she was staring at him.

"Something wrong?"

"Did you just pray for a new job?" she asked him.

"Yes, I was let go today," he said, handing her a plate.

"Why? What happened?" she questioned him with worry.

"They had to cut back on crews and I haven't been there as long as some of the other guys. So they had to let me go."

Honor put her fork down and stared at her plate.

"Don't worry. We've been in tight spots before and I'll find another job soon. Have faith. We'll get through it."

"Are we in trouble? Is that why Jerry didn't look happy? Are we going to have to move again? Should I get a job or something to help out?"

"Honor, honey, you don't need to worry about that. I'll get it figured out."

"Dad, you asked God to help us in our time of need... over our macaroni."

"I did. I asked the Lord for help financially. Not you," he assured her. "However, I request that you be patient and help cut back on things such as maybe reading the same books for awhile instead of wanting new ones and don't give me a hard time about having Mac 'n' cheese for dinner."

"Yeah, okay," Honor gave her father a smile. Then she picked up her fork.

CHAPTER 2

Will quietly snuck into Honor's bedroom. She was asleep and as usual she had fallen asleep with a book in her hand. He gently pulled the book from her hand and placed it on the nightstand. He then pulled a dog biscuit from his pocket and tucked it carefully under her pillow. He then walked back to the doorway and whistled softly. Finn ran into the room.

"Search boy," Will encouraged the dog to jump up on her bed.
Finn leaped on top of Honor. He sniffed around for the treat, nudging her from underneath her pillow.

"Oh come on, Finn." She looked at the dog as he ate his reward.

"Rise and shine," Will announced. "The chores won't do themselves."

"I have two weeks to get them done," she whined as she pulled the sheets over her head.

"Not if we aren't here." Will walked over and sat on the edge of the bed.

She rose from under the sheets. "What do you mean if we are not here? Where are we going to be?"

"Well I thought, seeing that we both have some time off. That maybe we should go and see your Grandma Jo."

"But you hate Alexberg."

"I don't hate it. It just..."

"Reminds you of Mom."

"You remind me too much of your mother. Alexberg just, well. I don't think I have been very fair to you, by keeping you from where she and I grew up."

"So, when are we going?"

"Soon, I want to be at Grandma's before dinner. So you and I need to get some stuff done before we leave."

Honor jumped out of bed. "Yeah! What do we need to do first?"

"The toilet."

"What?" Honor looked at her father in hope that he was joking.

"I just can't leave town knowing the toilet bowl hasn't been cleaned," he teased her with a serious look on his face as he walked out of her room.

Honor got out of bed and got dressed. She then grabbed a small suitcase from her closet and placed it on her bed.

"Dad, how long are we going to be at Grandma's?" she shouted from her room.

"Just a few days," he shouted back from the kitchen.

Honor began shuffling through her dresser and pulled out a random selection of clothes and stuffed them in the suitcase. She then went to her bookshelf and scanned her collection of books for something to read on their trip. She had them all arranged from the classics to the several books that were made into movies.

The movie books were her favorite because she loved to read the book before seeing the film with her father. It was another way she and her father could connect with the books she was reading.
Her love of reading must have come from her mother, she thought.

She had never known her mother because she had died giving birth to her. Her father talked mildly about her and the few memories that he had shared were of her reading and how he was amazed by how beautiful she looked when she sat quietly reading in her chair. The chair that now sat in the corner of Honor's bedroom.

Honor took a deep breath and pulled a wooden box from the top shelf. She sat down on the floor against her bed and opened the box. She pulled out a tattered book, ' The Adventures of Huckleberry Finn' by Mark Twain.

Her father had given it to her on her tenth birthday. It was the only book he had saved from his childhood. It was the book her mother had given to him when he was ten. She gently opened the cover and took out a photo he also had given to her. It was a copy of the one he kept on his bedside table. The photo was of her mother and father at ages nine and ten.

"Honor, breakfast!" Will called her to the kitchen.

"Okay," she shouted back.

She smiled and kissed her mother's picture. She then placed the photo back inside the cover, jumped to her feet and placed the book inside her suitcase.

~~~

Honor sat down at the table and stared at her cereal bowl. He had made oatmeal for breakfast again. She wished for something different. The reruns of the meals he has prepared lately, had her thinking that maybe her father really just didn't know how to cook. Only the basic meal in the box such as Oatmeal, Hamburger Helper, Mac 'n' cheese, and the occasional MRE, which tasted better than his disasters, when he did use a cookbook.

Will sat down across from her and bowed his head. "Heavenly Father, thank you for this day and the gifts you have given us. Please be with us as we travel today. Thank you for this meal we are about to eat. May it fill and nourish our bodies. Keep, guide and protect us. In your name. Amen."

Will looked at her as she blankly stirred her oatmeal. "Not too hot, is it?"

"No, it's okay," she answered him.

She took her spoon and smoothed her oatmeal until it was level. She then sliced her spoon through the cereal like a she was cutting a pizza. Will watched her as she carefully scooped up one of the triangle shaped lumps and proudly shuffled it into her mouth.

"What?" she asked when she noticed that her father was staring at her as she played with her food. Will just shook his head and ate his breakfast.

~~~

After breakfast Will went to his bedroom to pack his bag. He took a few of his neatly folded shirts from the dresser and laid them out on his bed. He then pulled out four pairs of socks and four pairs of boxers. He grabbed two pairs of denim jeans and two pairs of his cargo pants from his closet and placed them neatly inside his duffel bag. He finished packing his clothes, laying his shirts on top, inside the bag. He pulled the security box from the nightstand and placed it on the bed. He holstered his pistol and packed the box into his bag. Then walked out of his room.

He knocked on the bathroom door.

"Hey, are you almost finished in there? We need to get going soon if we want to make it there before dark."

"Yeah, just a minute," Honor said, with a mouth full of toothpaste as she spit into the sink.

"Hey, don't forget the toilet," he added.

"Yeah, okay," Honor rolled her eyes as she grabbed the toilet bowl cleaner from beneath the sink. She then squirted the cleaner into the bowl. She waited for the water to turn blue before she flushed the toilet. She grabbed her toothbrush, toothpaste, a few hair ties and her hairbrush. Will returned to the bathroom door as she opened the door.

"Did you use the toilet brush?"

"Dad, I know how to clean a toilet," Honor brushed passed him.

"Okay."

Will continued his way into the bathroom. He set out his toiletry bag and began gathering necessary items such as his toothbrush, toothpaste and deodorant and placed them in the bag. He then went to the medicine cabinet over the sink and took out a bottle of Ibuprofen and his bottle of Zoloft. He stuffed the bottle of Ibuprofen into the bag.

He opened the bottle of Zoloft and took out his daily doze and popped the medication into his mouth. He filled his water glass and chased the pills with a large gulp of water.

He stared at himself in the mirror for a moment. He brushed his long hair back with his fingers and took a deep breath. "Here we go," he said to himself. He tossed the prescription bottle into his bag and carried it out of the bathroom.

~~~

Will and Honor loaded their bags into the truck along with Finn's doggie bed. Honor was walking Finn around when Chelsey, the woman who lived in the apartment across from them, walked up to Will.

"Hey, you guys going somewhere?" she asked, smiling at Will.

"Yeah, we are going down see my mother for a few days," Will answered.

He had always enjoyed talking with Chelsey, but was nervous and almost clumsy around her because he had liked her from the day she moved in next door but never had the nerve to ask her out.

"Do you have to travel very far?"

"It's about three hours away."

Honor smiled as she watched her father and Chelsey stand there in an awkward pause of silence. She had encouraged him to meet someone, but he had always made up some excuse to not follow through on asking anyone out.

"Well, I hope you have a good trip. I'll keep an eye out for you while you're gone."

"I appreciate that. Thank you."

"Sure, I'll see you when you get back," she smiled at him. "Bye Honor."

"Bye," Honor waved as she opened the door for Finn to get into the truck.

Will started the engine. Honor buckled her seat belt and stared at him, catching him looking out his window as Chelsey went into the apartment building.

"She likes you, you know?"

"Who? Chelsey?"

"She has that look in her eye when she talks to you and she stares at you when you aren't looking. The same look you have now."

"I don't have a look."

"Yeah, you do!" she teased him.

"Why are you so observant on what people do, but you can't notice when it's time to clean your room?"

"It's hard to ignore the way some women drool over you."

"Drool? I don't think so."

"Well they do. You'd notice that too, if you weren't so worried about how clean my room is."

~~~

They traveled for several hours, only making the necessary stops using the restroom, grabbing snacks and letting Finn out to go to the bathroom. Honor spent most of the time reading and listening to her iPod. It was nearly five o'clock by the time they reached the small town of Alexberg.

Honor placed the bookmark inside her book and pulled the earbuds from her ears. She glanced out the window for a moment then turned her father.

"So what does Grandma do, I mean, for a job?"

"She's a writer."

"You mean she's an author?" she asked with excitement.

"Yes, she's an author."

"How come you never told me? Why don't I have any of her books?"

"Well, because she writes for adults."

"Like self-help books or something?"

"Yes... or something," Will hesitated.

Honor caught the tension in his voice. "Oh, like sex novels?" she giggled.

"What? No, honey, I'm uncomfortable with you using that word," Will cringed.

"Which one? Novel or sex?" She blurted out, just to watch him squirm again.

"You know which one."

"Sex?" she continued to tease him.

"Oh please, stop saying that word," Will cringed again.

"Why? What's wrong with it?"

"Because you are twelve and I am your father and I'm just not ready for this type of conversation."

"We are going to have this conversation eventually. I mean I already watched the video."

"I realize that. Wait, what video?"

"The one they show in fifth grade. Don't act so surprised. You did sign the paper on sex education so I could attend the class."

"I did?" he asked with a worried look on his face.

Honor nodded, "I don't really know why they called it sex education class. It really was a class where they separated the boys from the girls and showed us different videos on how our bodies change as we grow up. There wasn't anything really about sex at all."

"Honor, please let's talk about something else, I'm just not ready for all this right now."

"Then when?"

"How about your wedding night?"

"That would be awkward, wouldn't it? I mean, wouldn't I be with my husband at that point?"

"No because he will not exist."

"Then I wouldn't be married."

"Exactly!"

"Oh, so you are going to be one of those dads?"

"Yes, yes I am. No boys within ten, no, twenty feet of you."

"Seriously?"

"Yep," he smiled at her.

Honor opened her book back up for a moment. She looked back at her father.

"But wouldn't you want grand kids someday?"

"Wow, are you hungry? I bet you are cause you are talking crazy." Will pulled into the parking lot of the small town diner. "Let's stop here."

"But aren't we almost there?" she asked.

"Yes we are but we are stopping anyways," he said as he quickly parked the truck and turned off the engine.

Honor grabbed Finn's leash and hopped out of the truck. Will rolled down the windows of the truck as he waited for the dog to do his business.

"Good boy!" Will greeted Finn, welcoming him back into the truck. "We'll be back," he assured the dog as he shut and locked the truck door.

The waitress and other dinners turned their attention to the front door as Will and Honor walked in. Will gave a small nod as the people went on with their conversations.

"Take a seat anywhere. I'll be right with you," the waitress gestured.

"Thank you," Will responded as he led Honor to the nearest booth next to the window.

Honor placed her book on the table as he sat down in the booth facing the doorway. She stood for a moment looking around the diner till she saw the restroom sign hanging over a doorway near the back exit.

"I'm going to the bathroom, can you get me a Sprite?"

"Sure," he replied as he grabbed the menu that was wedged between the table condiments. Honor quickly walked toward the restrooms.

"Will?" asked a friendly voice. Will looked up from his menu.

"Annie?" Will stood up from the table.

"Oh my God, it is you. Wow, how have you been?" Annie hugged him tightly.

"Good, and you?" He pulled away from her.

"I'm doing good, real good. How's?" Annie paused for a second trying to remember his daughter's name.

"Honor," he quickly helped her. "She's great. She's right here."

Honor had walked up behind Annie. "Honor, this is Annie. We grew up together," Will introduced them. He couldn't keep his eyes off of her.

"Hi!" Honor smiled.

"Wow, you have grown. I haven't seen you since you were a baby," Annie smiled back at Honor.

"So, Annie, what are you doing in town, did you move back here?"

"No, I'm in Chicago now. Actually my sister, Val, is getting married in a couple of weeks so I came back a few days ago to help out with some of the final details."

"Valerie's getting married?" he sounded surprised.

"Yeah, I know right. So how about you two, what brings you home?"

"We just rolled into town, going to visit mom for a few days before heading back to the city."

"Are you still living in Des Moines?"

He nodded as he continued to stare into her eyes.

"I've meant to look you up every time I passed through. But never got around to it since I'm always on the go," She smiled noticing his continuous stare.

"What do you do?" He asked.

"I'm a personal organizer. People pay me to help organize their businesses and sometimes their personal life and homes."

"Sounds like fun. Do you get to travel a lot?"

"Yeah, but it's exhausting, so it's nice to get a few weeks off for the wedding."

Will nodded. Honor looked at Annie then at her father during a moment of silence. She noticed Annie nervously pulling her clothing gently and that she and her father were lost in staring at each other. She also noticed that there wasn't a ring on Annie's finger.

"Are you married?" Honor blurted out, breaking the silence between them.

"Honor, honey," Will looked at his daughter with a warning look.

"No, it's okay," she assured Will. "No, I'm not married."

"Do you want to join us?" Honor quickly responded as she shuffled over to make room for her to sit down.

"I'd love to, but I need to meet my sister here shortly. Maybe next time." Annie smiled at Will. "Will, it is really nice to see you again. I hope we can catch up soon."

"Yeah, I'll be around for a few days. You can stop by the house, if you want to."

"I just might do that. It was nice to meet you, Honor. Take care of your dad for me."

"I will." Honor smiled as she watched Annie walk toward the door.

"I like her," she said, as she turned back at her father. Will continued to watch Annie as she opened the door and walked outside.

"Wow, you've got it bad."

"What?"

"You couldn't be more evident, if you tried. You like her. Don't you?"

"We're just old friends."

~~~

The sun was setting as they entered a long driveway that was lined on both sides with tall trees. Beyond the trees on one side was a wide meadow that stretched out until it was lost over a hill. On the other side, sections of wooden fence ended as they saw a beautiful willow tree standing tall and looking over a small pond with a wooden dock. The tree's weeping branches glowed from the golden colors of the sun setting behind it.

They continued to drive slowly through the trees, which led to the house. Honor gazed out the window at the large house with a covered wrap around porch. Next to a small path, a garden grew with a white picketed fence protecting it from the free-range chickens emerging from a small coop, and picking at the ground around it.

Wind chimes hung beneath a petite tree in the front yard. They swayed softly, chiming to the rhythm of the calm, evening breeze. The sweet smell of lilacs filled the cab of the truck as they stopped in front of an old pole barn that had been converted into a garage.

"Is this where you grew up?"

"Yes, in fact, your great grandfather built it."

"Wow, it's so big," she grabbed Finn's leash as she opened her door. The dog quickly jumped out of the truck, nearly dragging her behind him.

"You can take him off the leash, he won't go anywhere."

"Yeah?" Honor unclipped Finn from the leash. The dog dashed around with his nose to the ground, his tail wagged wildly.

Will stretched as he too looked around. He sighed as he watched Finn ran from one spot to the next. "Let's see if Grandma Jo is inside."

He walked up to the front door and knocked. Honor followed as Will opened the door.

"Mom?" he called out. He could hear music playing softly.

"In here!" she shouted from another room.

Will continued through the house to the den. "Mom?" Will felt his face flush as he entered the den. His mother, Jo, had her back to the doorway. She was painting as her nude male model looked up from his pose at Will.

"Mom? What the...?"

"William," she looked over her shoulder briefly as she continued to finish her brush stroke. "Bradley, this is my son William. William this is Bradley," she casually introduced them.

Bradley stepped forward and held his hand out to Will.

"Sorry I'll shake it later..," he cleared his throat, "Your hand. When you're dressed." He looked away from the naked man and back to his mother who was still focused on her painting.

"Whoa!" Honor gasped from behind her father at the site of Bradley.

Will quickly covered her eyes with his hand and guided her back into the hallway. "Honey, please go back out on the porch," he continued to push her away from the den.

"Is that how grandma gets her inspiration for her books?" Honor asked.

"Mom!" He shouted over his shoulder. "Can I talk to you outside."

Jo put her brush into a jar of water.

"Bradley, lets finish at another time."

Bradley nodded as he started gathering his clothes from the couch. Jo walked out of the room and followed them outside.

"There she is," Jo quickly hugged her granddaughter and squeezed her tight against her breast. "My goodness, you have grown. What has he been feeding you?"

"Oatmeal," Honor struggled for air as she pulled away from her grandmother's large chest. Jo released Honor and turned towards Will.

"William, it's so good to see you," she placed her hands upon both sides of his face drawing him downward to kiss him on the cheek. "You're still so handsome, my son, and so strong and your hair! It's a wonder you're still single!" she smiled and wrapped her arms around him, pulling him down where she could hug him, "And you brought Finn." She looked down at the dog. He wagged his tail at the sound of his name. "I thought you two were coming on Saturday?"

"Maybe we should have, had I known you were entertaining," he pulled away, as Bradley walked out, now fully dressed. He nodded at Will and smiled at Honor who was giggling from behind Jo.

"Jo, just give me a call when you are ready to finish," Bradley said, as he walked down off of the porch. Will noticed how young the man was, now that he wasn't distracted by his nakedness.

"Will do Bradley, we'll talk soon." She waved at him as he got into his car.

23

"So just how old is he?" Will asked as he watched the young man drive away.

"Oh a few years older than you, why does it bother you? Your mother, having a naked man in her home?" she teased him.

"Well it's a little odd walking in on that. I thought you liked painting landscapes?"

"An artist has no boundaries," Jo announced proudly. "Besides it's on my bucket list to paint a nude portrait and Bradley is one of the models from the community college."

Will shook his head, "Okay."

"Enough about that. Will why don't you get your bags? Sweetheart, let's get Finn settled inside." Jo ordered them around as she put her arm around Honor. "We have so much to catch up on," she continued as they went inside.

Will walked back to the truck. He pulled their baggage from the bed of the truck and set them aside on the ground. He then grabbed Finn's bed and his dog food, and picked up both bags from the ground. He proceeded towards the front door. He juggled with the luggage, and as he was about to open the screen door, Finn ran at him from inside the house, pushing the door open. The screen popped out from the pressure of the dog's front paws.

"Finn, no!" Will shouted, stumbling backwards. As he tried to catch his balance, a cracking sound burst below his right foot. Everything dropped as his foot broke through a weak spot in the porch.

"Damn it!" he shouted.

Jo and Honor came running out.

"Whoa," Honor gasped at the sight of Will with his leg in the porch.

"William, are you okay?"

"No mom, I'm not," Will grumbled, pulling his foot out of the hole, and rubbing his now scraped up shin. "Honor, do you mind?" he motioned her to clear away the luggage, as he knelt by the hole. Honor pulled the bags away and she stepped near her father, the floorboards creaked and moaned beneath her feet.

Will studied one of the old, thin floorboards, "Dry rot. Mom, this decking is gonna have to go."

"I had no idea. How bad is it?"

"I don't know. By the looks of it, I may have to replace the whole deck." Will stood up and brushed himself off. He pulled out his phone from his pocket and took a few pictures of the deck.

"Well," Jo began helping with the bags. "There's not much we can do about it in the dark. Come on inside," Jo insisted.

~~~

Will sat at the kitchen with his tablet. He had uploaded the photos of the porch onto his construction app, and was drawing in the improvements.

"She's asking for you." Jo walked in from behind him, placing her hands on her son's shoulders.

"Yeah okay," He replied without breaking his focus on his new project. "Mom, I want you to look at this. I may have to replace the whole thing. What do you think about - " he held out the screen for her to see.

"William, you just do what you think is best," she interrupted him, paying no attention to the tablet as she sat down across from him.

"Mom, you didn't even look at it. I want you to be happy with it if I make these changes and make sure it's within your budget. "

"You know I'm not worried about my budget, and what's the rush son? You just got here. I didn't mean for you to come here to fix my porch."

"You need to get it taken care of before someone really gets hurt. And I might as well get it done while I'm here."

"You have the whole week and the weekend don't you?"

Will turned his eyes away from hers. "We're leaving early Friday morning. I have to get the rent paid, before Honor and I get kicked out."

"Friday? Oh, I guess I didn't realize how bad it was. I thought you were going to be here for the weekend at least."

"Yeah, well that's why we came today. Honor got some time off from school, and I thought we'd stay a few days, then head on home."

Jo sighed, giving him a stern look while crossing her arms.

"Mom, please. You know I didn't want to come in the first place."

"I know. I just thought you'd give home a try and not just leave so soon."

"You know I can't be here."

"William, it's been almost ten years. She'd want you and Honor. - "

"Don't Mom," he interrupted her "You know this is exactly why I didn't want to come." He stood up from his chair, "I should go check on Honor."

Will walked up the stairs and into the bedroom. Honor was sitting on the bed, her back against the headboard, reading. Finn lay at the foot of the bed. He lifted his head up when he saw Will entering the room.

"Hey, it's late. Come on…book down." Will spoke softly.

"Okay." Honor set her book on the nightstand and slipped her feet beneath the covers. Will walked over to the bed and tucked her in.

"Finn really likes it here. There's a lot of room for him to run."

Will nodded. "And what about you?"

"I love it too. I wish we could live here."

"Well, maybe we should visit more often."

"Really?"

"Yeah, we'll figure it out. Now get some sleep. Who knows what crazy things your grandma has planned for you tomorrow."

"Goodnight dad. I love you."

"Love you too, baby. Goodnight," he said as he kissed her forehead. He then switched off the light as he walked out of her room.

Will turned on the light in his bedroom. He sat down on the bed and removed his pistol from his holster. He held it in his hands for a moment then opened the drawer to his nightstand where he had put his security box. He unlocked the box and placed his pistol inside. He then pushed the drawer closed.

CHAPTER 3

It was dawn and the rooster crowed steadily, awaking Honor from her sleep. The curtains swayed with the fresh morning breeze coming from her open bedroom window. Finn was lying at the foot of her bed. He perked his head up as she arose from her pillow.

"Morning boy," she scratched him behind the ears. She threw back the bed sheet as she swept her feet to the floor.

Finn followed her as she made her way down the hallway. She peeked into her father's room. His bed had already been made up and he was nowhere to be seen.

She continued quietly down the stairs, the wooden floor beneath her bare feet creaked with every step. She admired the framed photographs that hung in the hallway leading towards the kitchen. She stopped and ran her fingertips along the edge of one of the frames. The picture was of her father and her mother sitting together, gazing into each other's eyes as if they were unaware of their being captured, their love frozen in time. Honor had seen photos of her parents before, but this one was her favorite.

Next to her parents was a photograph of her father in his Marine uniform, the traditional military picture of him standing alone in front of the American flag.

"Handsome, isn't he?" Jo approached her from behind. "Your father always looked handsome in his uniform. Just like your Grandpa." Jo pointed out the military photograph of her grandfather.

"Dad looks just like him."

"Yes, he does," Honor smiled as she continued to admire the other photos. "Grandma who is that?" she pointed to a picture of a young man leaning against a bright blue ford mustang.

"That's your uncle, Sethaniel. He's the one who took these pictures of your mother and father," she added as she admired the photos with Honor.

"He's a photographer?"

"Yes he is and a good one too. He's had a few of his photo's published in magazines."

"Does he live here in town?"

"No. He travels a lot, but sometimes he comes through town."

"How come dad doesn't talk about him?"

"Well, that is the question you should be asking your father."

"Where is dad anyway? He wasn't in his room."

"He got up early and went into town, to get the material for the porch." Jo smiled and brushed Honors wild hair back. "Are you hungry?"

"Yes. But I don't want any oatmeal."

"Good news. I'm out of oatmeal," she smiled. "I was just about to go out to the coop for some fresh eggs. Want to help?"

"Sure."

~~~

The town had just begun to stir. The town's folk gradually emerged from here and there. Store owners opened their shops as the morning commuters trickled through the main streets, some stopping for their morning coffee on their way to work. Three older gentlemen stood in front of the diner. They sipped on their coffee as they rambled, gossiping about this and that as they did every morning.

Will sat in his truck in front of the hardware store. He searched the job ads on his tablet as he waited for the store to open. Carl, the owner of the store and a long-time friend of his father's, recognized Will right away. He walked over to Will's truck.

"Well, if it ain't William McFadden," Carl tapped on Will's window. Will smiled. He set down his tablet and opened the door to the truck.

"Carl, how's it going?" He shook Carl's hand.

"Good, It's been a long time. You here visiting your mother?"

"Yeah, I'm here for a few days." Will answered, as he followed Carl to the store's entrance.

"And let me guess, she's got you fixing things?" Carl implied as he opened the door. "Got a list of what you need?"

"Yeah."

"Well, come on in," Carl turned on the lights and continued his routine. "So how's that daughter of yours? She's what? Nine now?"

"Twelve actually."

"Twelve. You'll soon have a teenager on your hands. Then the boyfriends start showing up."

"Don't remind me."

"Let's see that list of yours."

Will handed him the list from his pocket.

"Well, I know that I've got the screws and possibly the hardware, but the lumber, well I haven't had lumber for years, not since the mill shut down. I can order it and have it here in a few days."

Will looked discouraged. "I was hoping to get it done sooner than that."

"Well, I could still order it for you, but you'll have to pick it up in the city. I've got an old trailer you can use, if you want to do it that way."

"Yes, I think that will work," Will nodded.

"Alright." Carl picked up the phone.

Will walked around the store and gathered up some of the items from his list. Near the front wall next to the window he noticed a bulletin board. It was covered with help wanted flyers. All were asking for help in different areas around town: lawn care, remodels, landscaping and decks.

Carl hung up the phone. "Okay they're picking the order for you, and it'll be ready by one o'clock." Carl tore a piece of paper from his note pad. "Here's the address and number."

"Thanks. Say, why are there so many of these? Isn't there anyone that does construction around here?"

"Well, not so much here in town. Not since your father passed. Pastor Brock has done a few. But I have to tell you, he preaches better than he can swing a hammer," Carl laughed.

"You looking for some side work?"

"No. I mean yes, actually I'm in between jobs right now."

"Well, that whole bulletin board could keep a man busy the entire summer if you ask me. There are a lot of old houses out here, and good people willing to pay to get them fixed up."

~~~

Honor set the table as Jo stayed busy at the stove. The smell of fresh eggs and bacon filled the kitchen.

"Honor, honey could you get the orange juice and milk out?" Jo asked over her shoulder.

"Sure." Honor went to the refrigerator and pulled out the pitcher of juice and the half gallon milk.

"Boy, it's been a long time since I've had to cook for more than just me." Jo smiled at Honor as she scooped up the eggs into a serving bowl and placed the bowl on the table. "Oh I almost forgot, the biscuits." She hurried to the oven and pulled out the cookie sheet of golden brown biscuits.

"Smells good. What have you ladies been up to?" Will asked as he walked through the door making a beeline to the bacon on the table.

"Breakfast! Real breakfast!" Honor teased.

"I can see that," he grinned, snagging a piece of bacon.

Jo smacked his hand, making him drop the piece of bacon onto the table. "You know better than that. Go wash your hands. We need to say grace first."

Honor smiled and giggled. Will wrapped his arms around his daughter and hugged her tight.

"Did you wash your hands?"

"Yes," she pushed him away with a smile. He kissed the top of her head as he releasing her, then walked over to the sink and began lathering his hands with the soap.

"Were you able to find the stuff you need for the porch?"

"Yeah, but I have to go and pick up the lumber in the city later today." Will dried his hands. "Did you want to go with me sweetheart?" he asked Honor.

"Grandma and I were going to go to the bookstore today."

"Oh, I hope you don't mind. I told her we could go and pick out a few books since mine are a little adult for her."

"Sure. No problem. Just don't let her talk you into buying the whole store."

~~~

The warm sun shined brightly in the cloudless sky. Will had just returned from picking up the lumber. He unhitched the trailer and began to unload his tools.

Will set up his work area as Finn lay beneath a nearby tree, chewing on a stick. He began barking at a jeep making its way toward them. Will lifted his focus toward the jeep rolling along the gravel driveway.

"Finn, fuss!" He commanded the dog in German. Finn stopped barking and quickly ran to Will's side. "Platz." Finn laid down. Will tapped him on the nose. "Bleib."

Pastor Brock stopped his vehicle and smiled as he got out of the jeep. Brock is a tall strong man who was wearing blue jeans, a lightweight button-down shirt and flip-flops. He carried a brown paper bag as he approached Will.

"Well, I'll be." Brock greeted him with a handshake and a pat on the back. "I didn't know you were back in town. Haven't seen you since..." Brock paused a moment. He was going to remind him of when he had seen him last, but the look on Will's face made him change his words. "Well, it has been a long time. How are you?"

Will was a little taken aback. "Good, how about you?"

"I'm doing well, thank you. So how long are you here?"

"I'm just here for a few days."

"Well, I'll bet your mom is sure happy you are here. I see she put you to work?"

"Yeah well you know Jo. She can't be trusted with a hammer."

"Don't I know it," he laughed. "Is she around?"

"Ah, no, actually she is in town with Honor."

"I must have just missed her then. How is Honor?"

"Good, she's good."

"It's really good to see you, Will. Your Mom talks about you and your daughter quite a bit at church."

"My mother goes to church? When did that happen?"

"Well, she's been coming almost every Sunday for the last year and a half." Brock smiled. "You know, you and Honor should come to our Wednesday night. I'd love to meet her."

Will politely smiled but shook his head.

"I'm sure she'd enjoy it. There's worship and fellowship for the adults."

"Yeah, I don't know. I should really get this done before Friday. Maybe my mom could take Honor, if she wants to go."

"I hope to see you, if you decide to come."

Both men stood there for a moment in silence.

"Well I was out on my visitations and thought I'd come out and bring your mom some of the tea she likes. So if you could give this to her. I'd much appreciate it."

"No problem."

"Thank you and let me know if you need any help with the porch. I can be pretty handy with a hammer."

"I'll keep that in mind. Thank you!" Will smiled and shook his hand.

"Alright, well, I hope to see you around," Brock smiled.

CHAPTER 4

Will grabbed the towel hung on the hook as he stepped out of the shower. He had worked on the porch all day and he felt a sense of accomplishment. He began to dry himself off when he heard laughter coming from another part of the house. He walked into his bedroom with the towel around his waist, his chest and back still wet as he grabbed his clothes and quickly got dressed.

The laughter continued as he followed the giggles and chatter to his mother's bedroom.

"What's going on?" he asked. Honor and Jo became silent looking at each other as if they were keeping a secret. "Honor, it nearly nine o'clock. You should be in bed."

"Huh? Come on! I'm having fun. Just a little longer?" she pleaded.

"No, you know the rule, come on now. Lights out in five."

Honor rolled her eyes as she got up from the bed and hugged Jo. "Goodnight, Grandma."

"Goodnight, honey." Jo kissed her cheek. Honor walked past her father.

"Hey," he wrapped her up in his arms. "Goodnight, sweetheart. I love you." He kissed the top of her head.

Honor hugged him back. "Love you too." She walked out of the room.

Jo smiled. "You know, you really are a great father. She's lucky to have you."

"I'm trying my best. I think I'm the lucky one," he responded humbly.

"Son, how long has it been since you spent some time alone?"

"What are you talking about? I was alone practically all day."

"No, you were working the whole day and that's not what I mean," Jo smiled. "When was the last time you went out?"

"What, like out on a date?"

"Well, that too. Why don't you go out?"

"What, like right now?"

"Sure, why not?"

"What about Honor? If she wakes up and…"

"And nothing, William, tell you what, while you are here if you want to go out, go out," she smiled. "Have some fun!"

"By myself? That doesn't sound like much fun to me. I'll just grab a beer on the porch."

"Why don't you call Annie?"

"Okay, now I know what you two were giggling about."

"Call her."

"I don't have her number."

"Excuses. You know where her parents live."

"Mom, I'm not going to go over to her parents house this late."

"Well I'm not going to have you hanging around here when you have me to watch Honor. Besides I don't have any beer and don't you dare think about the Baileys in the fridge," she smiled.

Will sighed, smiling back. "Well I guess I could grab a beer at The Tavern."

Jo grabbed her wallet from her purse and pulled out two twenty-dollar bills. "Here it's is on me." She tried to hand the money to him.

"No, Mom, you don't have to do that," he said, refusing to take her money.

"Oh stop, think of it as payment for the work you did on the porch today." She grabbed his hand, placing the bills on his palm and closing his fingers around the money, "Now go."

Will shook his head at her and smiled. He knew he had to pick his battles with his mother, and when it was the ones that dealt with her generosity there was no winning.

~~~

Will sat alone at the bar. He stared blankly at the hockey game on the flat screen, nursing his cold beer. He paid no attention to the gentlemen glancing his way from the pool table on the other side. Will made eye contact with one of the men, who quickly averted his eyes away from him. Their faces were familiar, from high school maybe, but he couldn't remember their names. The noise from the hockey game and the other people cheering at the bar muffled their voices from across the room. Will felt uneasy. The men kept glancing at him and then turned away whenever he looked over in their direction.

Outside the bar Annie was walking on the sidewalk when she noticed Will in the window. She bit her lip and smiled as she watched him for a moment. She quietly walked into the bar.

"Hi," she nervously smiled at him.

"Hi. What are you doing here?" he asked.

"I was walking by and saw that you looked like you needed some company."

"Yeah, sure. Can I get you a beer or something?"

She smiled and sat down next to him. "Yeah, I'll have what you're drinking. I mean not your beer of course, but the same," she blushed another smile at him.

"I knew what you meant," he smiled back. "Excuse, another beer please," he requested of the bartender. The man behind the bar pulled a beer from the fridge and placed it in front of her, barely taking his eyes off of the game.

"Thank you," she politely nodded her head to the bartender.

"So how's it going with the wedding planning?"

Annie took a big gulp of her beer. "Good. Really great," she answered.

"You don't sound so sure."

"Okay, truthfully, it's awful! First of all, Val has now turned into a full-blown bridezilla. Nothing that she herself picked out is right. The dress is a size too small. So now, she is demanding everyone to practically diet with her. She would totally freak if she saw me drinking this beer. The DJ she picked out has canceled due to a friend of a friends cousin is having a Bar Mitzvah or something and he gets paid more at those things. My parents have been on my case cause I'm the only one of their daughters who is not in a steady relationship and they think I will never settle down and, oh, the cake. Val and her fiancée Greg, can't agree on anything. And I told her to, at least, let him pick it out cause she's not even going to eat much of it due to the fact that she is worried that her dress is going to burst at the seams if she even looks at food."

Annie took a deep breath and looked at Will. He had his bottle resting on his bottom lip, his eyes wide, with a puzzled look on his face. "Oh God, I'm boring you. Aren't I?"

"No, not at all," he smiled, taking a sip of his beer.

"I'm sorry. I needed to get away from all that chaos and here I am talking about it."

"No, really, it's okay. Vent. There's no need to hold it all in. Please continue," he contently focused on her.

She blushed and smiled, "You know, you really haven't changed much, have you?"

"What do you mean?"

"Just like when we were kids. It's so easy to talk to you and no matter what, you have this amazing listening superpower, and a strange willingness to listen to women rant on and on."

"Well, I do have a daughter so I am used to the drama."

Annie smiled again, this time looking deep into his blue eyes.

Will was a little taken by her gaze, "What?"

"Nothing," she continued to smile. "It's really nice to see you again. I had always thought about you since..." she looked down at her drink for a moment, then back at him. "You know I have this sudden craving for marshmallows."

"Marshmallows?" he gave her a strange look.

"Yeah, I have an idea. Do you want to get out of here?"

"Huh, yeah okay," he drank the last bit of his beer. He watched her chug her beer as he pulled out his wallet and set money on the counter.

~~~

Annie and Will drove to her house. He stayed in the truck as she quietly ran inside. A few moments later a light turned on in one of the upstairs bedroom windows.

Will could see her through the open curtain and tried to keep himself from watching her as she changed her shirt. The light soon turned off and in seconds she was out the front door and ran towards the truck carrying a fabric bag.

"Got it!" she cheerfully smiled at him as she jumped into the truck.

"Got what?"

"S'mores!" she replied holding the bag open to reveal the graham crackers, marshmallows and chocolate. "I had to hide these so my sister couldn't throw them out."

"S'mores? And how are we going to heat up the marshmallows?"

Annie dug out a lighter from her pocket and flicked it, "Just like the good old days!"

Will laughed. "Okay, then to the spillway?" he smiled.

"You read my mind," Annie grinned as she put her seat belt on.

~~~

Will backed into one of the parking spots facing the tailgate towards the spillway. Annie jumped out of the passenger's side with the bag in hand.

"Look at this sky! The stars are amazing," she gazed at the sky.

Will let down the tailgate and sat down on the gate as he watched her close her eyes. She breathed in deep and let it out with a sigh. She looked over at him. His piercing blue eyes held her stare for a moment before she walked over to him. He held his hand out, helping her onto the tailgate. Their legs dangled together as she set out the marshmallows, crackers and chocolate. Will leaped off the gate and rummaged the ground for a stick.

"Here you go," he said, as he handed her a stick, then sitting back down next to her.

"Thank you, so do you still like them burned?" she asked, as she stuck a marshmallow onto the stick.

"How do you remember these things?"

"I remember a lot of things, especially just being here-back in town. I mean, didn't you just feel this sudden burst of great memories flood your mind when you got back here?"

"Huh, no, not really. I really didn't want to come back in the first place," he said staring at his feet.

"Because of Becca?" she asked, trying to light the marshmallow on fire with the lighter.

"You know, I miss her. I miss her alot. And this town reminds me so much of her."

She looked over at him. He eyes glossy in the moonlight, she could see that the thought of losing Rebecca still remained fresh and deep as if it was only yesterday.

"I miss her too," she set down the lighter and placed her hand on his leg, she held the stick with the marshmallow in the other hand. She then rested her head on his shoulder.

He looked down at her hand. It had been a long time since he had felt such a soft gesture from a woman. He could smell the soft fragrance of lilac radiating from her skin. He quickly fought back the tears he has so desperately held in for years.

"I'm sorry," he placed his hand on top of hers and gave it a friendly squeeze as he lowered his head closer to hers. "I don't..."

She looked up at him; their lips now so close. She stared once again into his deep blue eyes just before she leaned into him and pressed her lips to his. He hesitated.

She felt his hesitation and embarrassment flushed into her cheeks, "I'm sorry." She leaned back from him.

"For what?"

"For making this awkward." She said in an outward breath as she made some space between them. She picked up the lighter and began to light the marshmallow again.

"It wasn't awkward," he said as he stood to his feet and walked in front of her. He smiled as he took the lighter from her hand and sat it onto the tailgate. "You just surprised me." He cupped his hands around her face and drew her close as he pressed his mouth to hers.

CHAPTER 5

The sunlight just began to tease the horizon. The morning dew clung to the tall grass that shimmered in the soft glow of dawn. Will parked his pickup truck and hurried into the house. Just as he was about to walk up the stairs his mother peeked out from the kitchen doorway.

"Did she offer you breakfast at least?" Jo smiled from behind her mug as she took a sip of the hot tea.

He nearly missed the first step, "What?"

"I know I told you to have fun, but coming home at dawn, now that sound like you had a bit too much fun," she teased him, walking out into the hallway.

"Mom, please. It's not like that. I wasn't."

"William, do you honestly believe that I thought you were at the bar this whole time?"

"We were just talking and lost track of time."

"We, as in Annie?"

"Yes."

"And how is Annie?"

"Good Mom, she's good," Will started his way up the stairs when she stopped him again.

"Well, aren't you going to tell me about your night?"

He leaned on the banister, "We talked pretty much all night. We fell asleep in the back of the truck. I took her home and that's it."

"That's it?"

"Yes Mom. That's it! Now please, don't tell Honor about last night and me coming home this morning, I don't need her to get any ideas."

"I will not lie if she asks, but I won't bring it up?"

"Thank you."

"Son, at least tell me one thing."

"What?"

"Did you have a good time?"

"Yeah, yeah I did," he smiled as he continued up the stairway.

~~~

Will stepped back from the porch and admired the completion of his hard work. He had just finished hanging a new porch swing and noticed no one was around to see it. It was quiet, Honor had been outside with him, but neither she nor Finn were to be seen. He grabbed his t-shirt and put it back on as he walked inside the house to look for her.

"Honor?" he called out as he climbed the stairs. He glanced in his mother's bedroom. She was asleep on her bed and was holding a glass of water that was slipping out of her hands. Will entered the room quietly. He was careful not to wake her as he took the glass from her restful grip. He set the glass down next to the small bottles of prescriptions sitting on the nightstand. He picked up one, which was an antidepressant.

Will glanced out the bedroom window when he had heard Finn barking outside. He set the bottle down back on the nightstand and left her room, quietly shutting the door behind him.

Will followed the sound of Finn's barking outside. Finn was standing on his hind legs with his front paws on the trunk of the willow tree. Will walked towards the tree and noticed Honor's legs dangling from beneath the branches.

"What'cha doing up there?" he asked his daughter who was sitting on one of the thick branches and leaning against the trunk just above Finn. She looked down at her father from behind her book.

"Reading with Mom," she handed down the photograph that she had brought from home.

"You know, you look just like her sitting up there. She sat in that very spot when she was your age."

"She did? This very branch?"

"Yep, she loved coming here to read. She was up there almost every day in the summertime." Will began to scale his way up the tree. The branches creaked beneath his weight. "Here, let me show you something."

Honor wedged her book between two thin branches and climbed higher along with her father to another large branch.

"Here," he pointed out an area on the trunk of the tree that had been stripped of its bark. The names Annie, Becca and Will were engraved together into the tree. The name Seth was also engraved, but just below the others.

Honor brushed her fingertip along her mother's name; then along her uncle's name.

"How come you don't ever tell me anything about Uncle Seth? Did he die or something?"

"No, he's still alive."

"How come I have never met him?"

"I don't know; we just don't talk anymore."

"Why not?"

"It's complicated."

"What so complicated about talking to your brother?"

Will shrugged his shoulders, then began to climb back down the tree. Honor followed him. She knew if she didn't ask, he'd never tell her.

"So, what's so complicated about talking to your own brother?" she asked again.

"Honey, sometime adults, especially guys, hold onto arguments. And because of those arguments they just stop talking, and before they know it time passes and you just don't know what to say to the other person." He tried to change the conversation, "Do you want to check out the new porch swing?" He pointed at the house.

"I know what you should say," Honor smiled trying to catch her father's eye contact. He continued to try to evade her by drawing focus on Finn.

"Hey, have you fed Finn lately?" he knelt down to the dog, scratching him behind the ears.

"Dad, I know what you should say," she said a little louder, getting him to finally look at her.

"I'm sorry," Honor suggested as she leaped from the lower tree branch onto the ground.

"Yeah, well, which one do you suppose should say that?"

"Both." She smiled again, "Then you say, 'I forgive you.'"

"It's that simple, huh?" he put his arm around her shoulders as they walked toward the house with Finn following behind them.

"So how long has it been since you last talked to him?" she asked curiously.

"Let's go see if your grandma want to see the new swing," he suggested.

"Dad!" Honor stopped in her tracks and crossed her arms at him. "Why do you always do that?"

"Do what?" he turned around, facing her.

"You always try to change the subject. And you never tell me anything that I want to know."

"Like what?"

"Like why you don't talk about Uncle Seth and why I have never met him. And why it upsets you to be here. Besides the fact it reminds you too much of mom," she took a deep breath and stared at him.

"Honor, honey, I don't know. I guess I'm just waiting until you are old enough to understand."

"Understand what? That my father is too scared to tell me the truth?"

"I'm not scared to tell you the truth. I... I just."

"What?"

"Look, a lot had happened in this town that I just don't want to think about anymore. The past is meant to stay in the past."

"Mom was in the past," Honor snapped as she fought back the tears. "So I guess you don't want to think about her either."

Before he could get another word in, she had run off toward the house.

"Honor!" he tried to catch her, but she ran into the house and up the stairs. She brushed past Jo at the top of the stairs.

"Honor, sweetheart, what's wrong?" Jo asked, as Honor stomped quickly passed her and into her room, slamming the door behind her.

"What was that all about?" Jo asked Will as he came through the door.

"She was asking about Seth and I - "

"You didn't tell her, did you?" Jo interrupted. "You know it was bound to come up. You can't hide from what happened between you and your brother."

"I know. She's just too young to understand."

"Maybe. But I think she is smart enough to try." Jo stepped down the stairs eye level with her son. "And maybe she can help you realize that it's time that you and Seth forgive one another." She patted him on the shoulder as she walked past him.

~~~

Will finished his shower and got dressed. He then packed his clothes back into his duffle bag. He was planning on heading home tomorrow and wanted to get an early start. He set aside pants, a shirt, underwear and a pair socks for the trip.

He walked out into the hallway. Finn was lying outside Honor's door.

"Honor?" he knocked on the closed door of her bedroom. She did not answer him. Finn sat up and looked at him. He waited for a moment; then knocked again softly, opening it just enough to peek in on her. She was lying on the bed with her back to the door. He walked into the room, letting Finn run ahead of him. The dog leaped onto the bed beside her. She didn't move. Will walked around to the other side of her. She was holding the picture of her mother trying her best to not look at her father.

"Hey, I'm sorry about earlier. Sometimes I don't think about your feelings when I get cornered like that with so many questions."

"Then why don't you just answer some of them?"

"Fair enough," he took a deep breath and sat down next her. "Okay, one question at a time."

"Really?" she asked, sitting up with excitement.

"Yes, really. What do you want to know?" he braced himself.

Honor took a moment to think. "I know mom died because of the car accident and that she had me just before she died. But you never really told me the whole story. Like, you know. The details of how it happened."

"You want to know the details of the day we lost her?"

Honor nodded her head.

Will took in a deep breath and let it out. "Okay."

CHAPTER 6
TWELVE YEARS AGO

Will staggered outside the bar and leaned against the brick wall. The alcohol had taken its toll on his motor skills as he fumbled with his phone. He tried to concentrate on the simple task of unlocking it.

He found the number he was looking for and hit send. The phone rang.

"Hey, it's Seth. You know what to do," the answering machine beeped.

"Hey Bro, where are you? I told you to pick me up at one. The bar is closing now. So call me back."

Will ended the call and took a seat on the curb. He put his head in his hands. Normally he did not drink as much as he did that night, but he was celebrating with his buddies after their second tour overseas. Not only did they all return home safely, Will was able to return to his beautiful wife in her last month of pregnancy.

All his buddies had left about a half an hour ago. They were on their way to the city for more partying and Will stayed behind hoping his little brother was coming to take him home safely.

He took a deep breath as the last few patrons staggered from the bar and walked down the street.

He looked at his phone, scrolled to Becca's name and hit call.

"Will is everything okay?" Becca answered, her voice soft and gentle.

"Yeah, I'm fine. Hun, Seth didn't show up and the guys have already taken off and - "

"You need a ride," she finished his sentence.

"Yes. I know it's late. Do you feel up to driving?"

"Yes I will come and get you. I can't sleep anyway. The baby is kicking up a storm. I think she knew her Daddy needed a ride."

"You mean HE knows his old man needs a ride."

"Oh now I know you drank too much, cause you know she going to be a girl," she teased him. "I hope you saved some cash, cause I have a craving for peanut butter and chocolate, so if you happen to wander over to the Casey's..."

"Say no more. Peanut Butter cups it is."

"I love the way you think. I'll see you in a few."

"Hey Becca, I love you."

"You better," she laughed. "I love you too. See you in a bit."

Will smiled as he carefully got up from the curb. He still felt the buzz as he walked across the street to the convenience store.

~~~

He purchased a King Size package of Peanut Butter Cups and a Red Bull. He then walked back outside and sat down on the curb. It was a cool summer night and the moisture in the air from the muggy day before started to dampen his clothes.

He had finished his sixteen-ounce can of Red Bull as he waited. He pulled his phone from his pocket and called her again. It rang a few times then went to voicemail. He hit end; then called her again.

A siren erupted the quiet street as a fire truck blared past, turning on Willow Avenue with it's lights flashing. Will looked at the clock on his phone. A chill ran down his spine as he worried about where Becca was. Another siren and more flashing lights whizzed by him. This time, the local Sheriff and another squad car sped past and down the street.

Will jumped to his feet and ran after the emergency vehicles down the street.

Will's heart raced as he approached an accident scene. The firetruck and police cars with lights flashing eliminated the darkness of the road and reflected off the faces of the first responders.

There was a dead mangled deer lying in the middle of the road and a car with its hood and front end hugging a roadside tree. Rebecca's car!

"BECCA!" Will screamed as he pushed himself into the crowd of fireman and medical personnel.

"Sir, please stay back!" the Sheriff warned as he grabbed him, pulling him away from the car.

"That's my wife!" Will struggled with the officer. "Becca!" he shouted to her as he shoved the officer. "Let me go!" he demanded.

"Hey, let him go," Pastor Brock, the fire house chaplain shouted as he ran over to the men. "I got him."

The officer released Will. Will continued to get as close as he could. Pastor Brock followed close behind.

The firemen were using the Jaws of Life to get her door open. Rebecca's eyes were closed and she had a neck brace on. A medic was leaning over her from the back seat of the passenger's side.

Brock put his hand on Will's shoulder. "Come on, let's give them room." He guided him back.

Will felt an overwhelming burn in his throat as he ran behind one of the nearby police cars. Brock placed his hand on Will's back as Will vomited next to the car.

"Breath. Take a deep breath. I need you to stay calm."

"The baby," Will looked up at Brock, wiping his bottom lip with the back of his hand. "Is the baby okay?"

"They said they had a heart beat —"

"Okay, that's it! Let's go!" One of the firemen shouted as they removed the door. "Let's get her out of there." The medical crew, who were standing by, rushed over with their gurney.

Will walked closer and watched as they carefully pulled Rebecca out of the car. They guided her gently onto a board, strapping her securely to it, then carried her to the gurney and towards the ambulance.

Will raced over to her, "Becca! Baby, I'm here!" He tried anxiously to get closer to her but was unable to reach her as they rushed her into the back of the ambulance.

"Can I go with her?" Will asked the man shutting the back door.

"There's no room, please step back."

"William, I'll take you," Brock offered, guiding him to his car.

~ ~ ~

Will sat silently in the emergency waiting room. He was not allowed to see his wife when they brought her in. Minutes felt like hours as he watched medical staff walk in and out of the double doors that lead down the hallway. Each time the door would open he tried to see what was going on.

"Any word yet?" Brock asked as he sat down next to him. He tried handing him a cup of coffee.

"No," Will refused the coffee. "No one is telling me what's going on. I can't just sit here." He stood up from his seat and paced back and forth.

"William," Jo shouted as soon as she entered the waiting room. "Becca? Where is she? Are you okay? The baby, how's the baby?" She frantically asked.

"I don't know anything yet."

"Mr. McFadden?" the doctor came out into the waiting room. The tone in his voice and the look on his face gave Will a chill.

Will looked at him and shook his head.

"I'm sorry, we did all we could. She coded and we just couldn't get her back."

Will shook his head, "You gotta keep trying, get back in there. You have to try!" Will pleaded with him.

"I'm very sorry, sir, she's gone," the doctor said.

"No, she's not," Will fell to his knees and held his head in his hands as his body trembled. "She can't be," he sobbed.

His mother knelt down and tried to comfort him. She wrapped her arms around him as she looked back up at the doctor. "The baby? What about the baby?"

"She's doing well. We had to do a cesarean, which was successful," the doctor assured them. "She was a little stressed but she is stable. They took her up to the intensive care unit."

"It's a girl?" Will managed to ask.

"Yes. Would you like to meet your daughter?"

Will silently nodded.

Jo put her arm around her son as a nurse lead them to the intensive care unit on the maternity floor. Will could hear laughter and joyful conversation in the rooms he passed. The voices haunted him as he tried not to think that that was supposed to be his family in those rooms- enjoying the birth of his daughter with Becca and their family and friends. But she was gone and the excitement had been overtaken with grief.

Will touched his fingertips to the glass of the window. He stared at the tiny baby, swaddled in a pink blanket, asleep in a transparent plastic bassinet that was marked 'McFadden'. She had soft mocha skin and black curly hair that peeked out of the little pink hat that covered her head.

"She's beautiful, William, just beautiful," Jo gasped.

"Like Becca." Will stepped away from the window. "Excuse me," he turned quickly and walked down the hallway.

"William!" Jo shouted out to him as she watched him disappear down the hall.

~~~

Will wandered into the stairwell, where he collapsed along the wall. Trembling, he buried his head in his arms against his knees as he tried to keep his sobbing under his breath.

His attempted to contain it failed when he wailed loudly, his mournful cry echoing throughout the stairwell.

He sniffled as he heard a door open from one of the floors and voices entering the stairwell above him. He picked himself up, wiped his face and walked down to the main floor and exited the stairwell before they could see him.

He made his way back to the emergency waiting room.

"Will!" a familiar voice called out to him from behind.

Will turned to see his brother standing by the nurse's station. Will's face grew warm at the site of his brother. His blood boiled in his veins as he quickly lunged toward him.

"Where the hell were you?" Will shouted as he grabbed his brother by the shirt and threw him up against the wall.

"Will. I... I was," Seth stood still in his brother's grasp. "I forgot."

"Forgot? No, I'll tell you what you forgot." Will slammed his brother against the wall again. "You forgot the one thing, the one thing I asked of you and now she's gone because of you."

Seth averted his bloodshot eyes, "Man I'm sorry. I...I just."

Will gritted his teeth and stared into his brother's blood shot eyes.

"You're high, aren't you?" Will snapped at him "Aren't you?" Will's hand balled into a fist and before he could think about it, he punched Seth in the jaw. Seth winced, grasped his face as he hit the ground. Blood poured from his mouth staining the front of his shirt.

"William!" Brock ran into the room toward the two men. He pulled Will away from his brother; then assisted Seth to his feet.

"Get out of here!" Will shouted at his brother as he lunged at him again.

Brock quickly put himself between the brothers, his hands extended out toward Will. "Seth, why don't you go and get cleaned up? Have a nurse look at that."

"Whatever," Seth glared at his brother as he walked away. Brock held Will back.

"Let go of me," he snapped. "I don't need you here either." Will pushed him away.

"William, you need to calm down. Going after Seth isn't going to solve anything. It's not going to bring her back. He's your brother."

"I have no brother."

CHAPTER 7

Is everything okay?" Jo asked. She sat in her new swing with a blanket over her shoulders and was sipping on some hot tea.

"Yeah," Will quietly answered as he leaned against one of the columns of the porch, looking out at the willow tree. Its long leaves shimmered, reflecting the moonlight. He sighed.

"Can't get a view like this in the city," Jo commented.

"No you can't," Will sat down on the steps.

"You know, you really don't have to hurry back to Des Moines. Honor told me she didn't have school for another week."

Will smirked, "Did she happen to tell you why she didn't have school?"

"Yes and I am proud of her for sticking up for herself."

"Well, she almost broke that poor girl's wrist. I shouldn't have taught her those moves."

"Don't be so hard on yourself. You did what any father would do. It's good that you teach her things like that." Jo smiled. "You're a good father and that girl loves you."

"I just wish I could do more. I need to find a job so I can give her everything she deserves."

"Have you thought about starting your own business here?"

"No, I don't think that would work."

"William, just hear me out. You have the job skills and the know how to run things. I could be a silent investor to get you started with whatever you need: insurance, advertising, tools-you name it!"

Will shook his head. "Mom I don't think this town could support a small business like that."

"Of course it could. Carl's wall is full of help wanted flyers and when you're done with those, you can expand to the surrounding towns. Not to mention, you'll have the availability to travel when you need to and I can help take care of Honor."

"I can't take Honor away from her school and her friends. It wouldn't be fair for her."

"Oh pish posh. When was the last time she asked if a friend could come over or the last time she went to a sleep-over?"

Will thought for a moment, "I don't know."

"She's happy here. You can enroll her at the school here. You both can have a clean slate."

"Mom, you know, I don't want to be here: in this town."

"William, you are going to miss her either way. You can't live your life avoiding things that remind you of Becca."

"I know that. It's not just her, it's the town."

"Poppycock," Jo snapped at him. "You are just like your father when it comes to the truth. How long do you think it's going to take for you to realize the path God has set before you?"

"What?"

"He has opened a door for you William. All you have to do is walk through it." Jo smiled. "It's your time right now, to do what you really want. If you are willing to allow me to help you."

Will took a deep breath. He knew she was right. He had run out of money and options. And he knew deep down, that Honor wasn't happy at school. Maybe this was an open door that God had opened up for him. This was a fresh start, a chance to get back on his feet and work his way up.

"Are you sure about this, me and Honor living here?"

"Absolutely!" Jo smiled.

"Okay," he smiled back, "but under some conditions."

"Okay."

"First, you can't pay for everything. Second, Honor has to do chores. She's not a guest if we live here. So please don't do things for her all the time. And last, please no more naked men."

~~~

Will stopped at the gas station. He opened the gas cap and began to fill the tank when he noticed, Annie, walking toward him. She did not notice him staring at her, as she walked across the street. She was arguing with somebody on her cell phone. He couldn't help himself as he laughed when he noticed how cute she looked, even though she looked upset. She walked with the phone to her ear with one hand, and gesturing wildly, swinging a small plastic bag with her other hand.

"Look, I can't talk to you right now!" she stopped on the sidewalk in front of the gas station.

Will watched her as she continued to shout on the phone.

"No! I told you I can't talk to you about it right now. No, you are not listening. I'm hanging up now!" she hung up on the person.

"Someone upset about their closet?" Will teased her, as he walked up behind her.

Annie turned around, "Will? Hey, you startled me."

"Sorry. Is everything okay?"

"Yeah, just a misunderstanding, this person is completely out of their mind," she smiled.

"I'll bet. I wouldn't want to argue with you either," he grinned.

"Hahaha! So what are you up to today, besides sneaking up on people?"

"Road trip."

"Really? Where? Is Honor with you?"

"No, she stayed at the house with my mom. She needed to help make some room for our stuff."

Annie looked at the trailer behind his truck. "You're moving back home?"

Will nodded, as he walked back to the pump. "Mom convinced me to move in with her for awhile."

Annie followed him, "Really? William McFadden, moving back home? Wow, what's next?"

"Maybe start my own business."

"Well good for you," she smiled. "So, are you going to move all your stuff by yourself?" She asked in such a way, as if she was hinting for him to invite her.

"I'll be alright, there's not much, just some boxes and some furniture," he looked at her, as she looked at him then at the truck. "Do you want to come along? Unless you had some wedding stuff, you have to do?" He pointed at the bag in her hand.

"Huh, no, this," she blushed, as she stuffed the small bag into her purse. "Val doesn't need me today. I'd love to come."

"Great, I just need to run inside to pay, then we can go," he smiled as he pulled his wallet from his back pocket.

"Yeah, I need to use the restroom anyway," she said, as she followed him inside the gas station.

Annie walked to the bathroom and locked the door behind her. Will walked over to the glass cooler. He grabbed a couple bottles of water, then walked over to the cashier. He paid for his gas and beverages and then walked outside to his truck.

Annie stood in front of the mirror, her hands gripping the porcelain sink. She took a deep breath, as she looked at the clock on her phone. She then nervously turned toward the top of toilet, where she had place the pregnancy test she had just taken. "Oh, thank you, Lord," she said out loud as she read the negative result. She tossed the test into the trash and washed her hands.

Will was sitting in his truck when Annie came out of the station. She smiled at him, as she ran over to the passenger's side and got into the truck.

"Everything alright?" he asked her.

"Everything is perfect," she smiled as she handed him a package of Twizzlers. "Can't have a road trip without licorice."

He laughed, "Now all we need is to do is listen to Bohemian Rhapsody on way."

"I have the soundtrack on my iPod," she grinned, as she buckled her seat belt.

~~~

Honor ran her fingertips along the binding of the books on one of the many large bookshelves in her grandmother's den. She pulled out a book titled 'Becca's Dance'.

"Who's Jordyn Merlyl?" Honor asked Jo, as she entered the room holding a mug of hot tea.

"Who do you think she is?" Jo smiles, as she points to the back of the book. Honor's eyes lit up as she saw her grandmother's photo on the back cover.

"Is it about my mother?"

"No, but I thought Becca was a beautiful name, so I used it for my main character."

"Can I read it?" she asked, as she read the back.

"No, I think that one might be a bit too spicy for you. Plus I would never hear the end of it, if your father found out I let you read one of my novels at your age."

"Oh, so there's a lot of sex in it, huh?" Honor replied, as she placed the book back into it's spot on the shelf.

"Let's just say it has just the right amount of spice to keep it interesting."

Honor continued to look at the books on the shelf, till she pulled another one out.

"Who is Sue Raymond? She has so many."

"She's a local author, like me. She writes inspirational, mystery and fantasy," Jo smiled. "She's a great writer, just you watch, she'll be on the New York's Best Sellers List soon. Next to me of course," Jo sat down in the chair next to the window. "Why don't you try 'Healer of Surflex By Lady Laindora."

"This one?" Honor pulled out the one with a dragon on the cover.

"Yes, I think you'll like that one," Jo sipped on her tea, as she gazed out the window. The clouds had covered the sunlight and thunder rumbled in the distance. "It looks like a big storm is coming in."

Honor walked over to the window. "Look at those clouds over there," she pointed out a dark shelf cloud coming from the west. "I hope dad doesn't have to drive through this."

"Let's check the weather report. Then we can call your dad and see if he made it there okay."

~~~

Will and Annie had just arrived into the Des Moines area when Will was wrapping up a call from Honor.

"I love you too, sweetheart," Will said to her. "Make sure Finn is inside, you know how nervous he gets during storms...Yes I won't forget...Okay love you, bye." Will ended the call. "Sounds like there is a storm coming in. Honor said it's heading our way," he said to Annie.

"Do you think we'll make it back tonight?" she asked.

"No. The way it sounds we may have to pack the trailer tomorrow morning," Will stopped the truck in front of his apartment and turned off the ignition. "I'm sorry, I should have checked the weather before I invited you along. I don't want to make you late for anything tomorrow."

"That's okay. I don't really need to do anything until Monday," she assured him.

"Well, this is it." Will said as he got out of the truck and stretched.

Annie hopped out of the truck and followed him into the apartment. Will unlocked the door and opened it. An envelope was on the floor, under the door. Will picked it up and opened it. EVICTION NOTICE was printed at the top of the letter inside. Will crumpled it up quickly and threw it away in the trash.

"What is it?" she asked him, as she closed the door behind them.

"Nothing. It doesn't matter now." Will threw his keys onto the table and proceeded to walk through the apartment. "I have some boxes in the closet. We can get everything packed so we can leave first thing in the morning," he said in an orderly tone.

She noticed the change in his voice. She waited for him to leave the room before she peeked at the letter he had tossed in the trash. She read it quickly then placed it back in the trashcan. She walked into his room, where he was folding a pile of boxes he had pulled from his closet. He was getting frustrated as he tried to secure them with packing tape.

"It looks like you've done this a few times," she commented.

"Yeah, well that is why we don't own much. It's easier to move," Will said loudly, continued to struggle with packing tape.

She could see the frustration and the anxiety in his eyes. "Will, here let me help you." She walked over to him taking the mangled tape dispenser from him. Their hands touched. He took a deep breath as he held her hand.

"I'm sorry, I just," Will tried to calm down. He looked into her eyes as she looked back at him. "I don't mean to be rude. I just didn't really want to move in the first place. And now I'm really feeling forced and rushed into it."

"The letter?" she asked in a gentle voice.

Will nodded. She gave him a short smile. "No one is rushing you. You have plenty of time. Now why don't you let me fold the boxes and you can worry about dinner. I like pepperoni," she ordered, as she pushed him from behind, out of the room.

"Did you just take over?" He turned around, making her hands slide from his back and onto his chest. She retracted her hands from him but he grabbed them quickly and pulled her to him.

"Yes, yes I did. That is what I do," she responded, surprised by his gesture. "Now if you want my help I'm - "

He quickly interrupted her by placing his lips onto hers. He kissed her softly. "You're something else, you know that," he said as he drew himself away from her. He walked toward the front door, grabbing his keys from the table and leaving her frozen from his kiss and a smile on her face.

~~~

The clouds started to swallow the sunlight when Will returned. Chelsey had just walked out of her apartment as he entered the front door. He was juggling with the pizza box, a six-pack of beer and a paper bag of groceries.

"Let me help you with that." She rushed to his aid, grabbing the bag just as he was about to drop it onto the floor.

"Thanks," he smiled at her.

"I didn't think you guys were going to be back so soon," she smiled as she carried the bag to the door for him.

"Uh, we're not really back," he paused outside the door. "I actually decided to move back home."

"Oh, okay," she said with disappointment. "Do you need any help?"

"No, I think we can manage," he smiled.

"Will?" Annie opened the apartment door when she heard voices in the hallway.

"Oh, I'm sorry I didn't know you had company," Chelsey blushed, she felt awkward when she saw Annie.

"Annie, this is Chelsey, my neighbor. Chelsey this is Annie," he introduced them.

"Hi."

"Nice to meet you." Annie stepped into the hallway.

"You too," Chelsey shook her hand.

"Will and I grew up together," Annie looked at Will. The three of them stood there for a moment in silence.

"Well, I should go. You too look like you have an evening planned," Chelsey said handing the bag to Annie.

"Did you want to join us? We've got plenty," Annie invited her.

"Oh no, I was just on my way out to meet up with some friends," she answered quickly. "It was nice to meet you. Will tell Honor hi for me. And keep in touch."

"Yeah, I will. Bye." Will watched her walk away then looked at Annie. She smiled at him as they walked into the apartment. "What?"

"She's cute. Did you guys ever..."

"No," he blushed a little. "We are just neighbors." He set the pizza and beer on the counter.

"I saw the way she looked at you. How come you two never hooked up?" she teased him.

"Because she lives next door. And if it didn't work out then it would have been very awkward and complicated."

Annie laughed, "So you did think about it?"

"Of course I did," he grinned as he gently grabbed her arm and pulled her to him. "And it's a good thing I didn't act on it, because then I might not be here with you now."

"Good point," she kissed him on the cheek and playfully pushed him away. "I'm starving. Let's eat."

~~~

Honor walked barefoot, outside with Finn. The storm had passed and the light from the sunset casted a rainbow across the sky. Branches and leaves were scattered on the ground, as she walked cautiously on the wet grass. Finn ran around with his nose to the ground.

"Finn!" she called for him, as she threw a stick out in front of him. He dashed after it and quickly returned with it, dropping it at her feet. He stared at it and wagged his tail as she threw it again.

Finn stopped just before he reached the stick as he saw a Volkswagen van coming up the driveway. His ears stuck straight up and he began to bark, Honor ran over to him and grabbed him by his collar.

Honor watched as the man driving the van, waved at her, as he stopped the van in front of the house. She gave him a short smile when she recognized him from the photographs on her grandmother's wall.

"Finn, sit," she commanded him, as she watched the man pull a duffle bag and a camera bag out from the back seat.

"Hi," he smiled. "You've grown up since I last saw you. Do you remember who I am?" he asked, as he walked up to her, flinging the camera bag over his shoulder.

Honor nodded. "Uncle Seth," she answered.

"That's right. And who is this?" Seth asked as he set his bag on the ground. He knelt down and put his hand out for Finn to smell him.

"This is Finn."

"Like Huckleberry Finn?"

Honor nodded, "How'd you know?"

"Well, it was one of our favorite books growing up. He's beautiful dog," he pet Finn under the chin. "Is Jo and your dad here?"

"Grandma is inside. Dad won't be back until tomorrow. We're moving in with Grandma. So he went to get our stuff," Honor smiled.

"Is that so?" Seth asked.

Honor nodded.

"Okay, well, you know what that means, don't you?" he grinned.

Honor shook her head.

"That means you and I can catch up before your grumpy old dad gets back," he stood and picked up his bag. "Come on, let's go find your grandma."

~~~

Annie jumped as the thunder cracked loudly, shaking the room. The wind blew and the rain tapped on the bedroom windows. She sighed as she turned onto her side, facing the door. Shadows of the stacked boxes in Honors bedroom danced along the walls as lightning lit the room. She could hear Will moan from his room. She tossed the sheets off of herself and slowly got out of the bed. She straighten the t-shirt Will had loaned her to sleep in, one of his Marine t-shirts, that surrounded her with his scent. Quietly she opened the door and walked down the hallway. He moaned again as she entered his room. He breathed heavily, as he laid on his back, bare chested with boxers, and sheets were tangled between his legs from his restless sleep.

Annie crawled onto the bed next to him. She laid her head onto the pillow, facing him. She watched his chest rise and fall, as he breathed. She traced his tattoo on his arm with her fingertips. He moaned and his body twitched. She placed her hand on his chest. "Will," she woke him gently.

Will touched her hand and opened his eyes, "Hey, you okay?"

"I'm fine. You looked like you were having a bad dream."

"No, I just don't sleep well."

"I can leave, if you want me to?"

"No, it's okay," he straightened the tangled sheet from his legs and welcomed her beneath the covers with him. "I didn't wake you, did I?"

"No," she closed the space between them, and rested her head onto his chest. "You were moaning pretty loud though. What were you dreaming about?"

"Nothing really."

Will kissed her forehead as he stroked her arm. Annie smiled as she tilted her head up and kissed him. He returned the kiss and wrapped his arms around her and drew her closer. She leaned on his chest and glided one hand behind his neck and the other down his chest. He stopped kissing her and inched his hips away and stopped her hand before it traveled beneath the sheets.

"I'm sorry. Did I do something?" she asked.

"No, you're fine. I just don't want to do anything we might regret."

"Regret?" she pulled away from him. "Will, you are sending me mixed signals. I thought that this is what you wanted."

"I do, believe me. I want this," he sat up and stared into her eyes. "I just don't want the same thing we did after Becca died to happen again."

"Will, that was a long time ago," she sat up. "We were both grieving."

"I know that."

"I guess we never really talked about it. Did we?" she gazed at him.

"No, we didn't talk about it cause you just left," he said firmly.

"Is that why?" Annie adverted her eyes away from him. "My best friend had just died and ... and we just moved too fast. I needed some time to think."

"Some time to think is a week maybe two. But you didn't call, you kinda just disappeared."

"I know and I'm sorry. I wanted to call. But I didn't know what to say. I thought that what we did was just out of grieve and that it didn't mean anything."

"It did mean something, it just didn't happen at the right time I guess."

"Do you want to talk about it now?"

"I don't know. I mean, what are we doing? Is this just a fling, like before?"

"I wouldn't call it a fling. Just two really good friends enjoying each others company."

"So, friends with benefits?" he asked with disappointment.

"Well, when you say it like that, it sounds awful," she disagreed. "More like intimate best friends."

"That's the same thing," he shook his head.

"Will, why do we have to call it anything? Why can't we just have fun together?"

"Because I want more than just having fun."

"More as in a relationship?" she asked. He nodded.

"Annie, what's going to happen after your sister's wedding? I mean are we just going to go our separate ways like before?"

"I don't know, I never really thought that far."

"Well I have." He took her by the hand. "These last few days with you have been amazing. The way we connected from the start, as if the years we had apart never existed. I want to be with you. Not just intimate best friends. Even if we have to have a long distant relationship I'm willing to make it work."

Annie's eyes began to water. "What's wrong? Why are you crying?" he asked her as he pulled her into her arms.

"I don't know," she sniffled. "It's just been so long since I had someone who felt the same way. Will, I want to be with you too, even if it means taking it slow. I want to give us a chance."

Will smiled as he leaned toward her. He kissed her lips with excitement. They embraced and laid back down on the bed. She paused for a moment, "Did we just make it official?"

"I think so. If that's alright with you," he grinned as he pressed his lips against hers. And wrapped his arms around her.

She gently pushed him back. "Taking it slow, right?" she interrupted him with a giggle.

"I guess we should get so sleep then," he kissed her again.

"Goodnight," she said as she turned to her side with her back toward him and got comfortable. He followed her gesture as he wrapped his arms around her, resting his head on the pillow next hers as he hugged her from behind and closed his eyes.

CHAPTER 8

It was about noon, when Will and Annie returned to Alexberg. Will stopped the truck on the street, in front of her parent's house.

"Thank you again for coming along."

"Your welcome. Are you sure you don't want me to come with you to help unload?"

"No. I think Honor and I can get it."

"Okay. I'll see you later then?" she smiled.

"Yeah, I'll call you, or you call me"

She opened the door and got out of the truck. She shut the door then leaned inside the window. "Since we are taking it slow, perhaps we should start with a proper date," she smiled.

"Okay, what do you have in mind?"

"A wedding."

"Are you asking me to your sister's wedding?"

"Yes. I would love for you to be my date. You can bring Honor," she added, trying to convince him to go.

"She would love that. So yes," he smiled back at her. "I'll have to take her out to get something to wear."

"I could take her. I mean if that's okay with you?"

"You know, that would be great. She'd probably enjoy shopping with you over me. I'm not very good in the dress up department."

"I could take her tomorrow afternoon?"

"Okay," he smiled. "I can drop her off after church."

"Great. Just give me a call." Annie smiled.

"I will," he smiled back.

~~~

Finn ran toward Will as he was getting out of the truck.

"Hey Finn!" He knelt down to welcome the excited dog in his arms. Finn's tail wagged with delight as he flopped on the ground for Will to pet him and rub his belly.

"Dad!" Honor shouted from the front door and ran to him. She too was excited to see him as she leaped into his arms. "I missed you."

"I missed you too," he kissed her on top of her head. "I hope you were good for your grandma."

"Uncle Seth is here!" she pointed toward the house. Will looked at the front door as Seth walked out onto the porch.

"He showed me his portfolio of the photographs he had taken all over the country. And he's back now. He's going to Valerie's wedding. And he asked me if I would be his date." Honor rambled on.

Will continued to stare at his brother, who was staring back at him.

"Sweetheart, you can't go with him," Will informed her, as he continued to stare.

"Dad, why not?" She was disappointed.

He looked at her and smiled. "Because you are going to be going with me. Annie invited us already. She's going to take you shopping tomorrow to find something to wear."

"Really?" she asked with a big smile.

Will nodded.

"Awesome!" she hugged him.

"Now, why don't you help me take some boxes inside," he handed her a box as he begun to unload the truck.

Seth walked slowly from the porch toward Will's truck.

"Seth, guess what? Dad said that we are going to the wedding too." She smiled as she walked passed him.

"That's great." Seth smiled back. "Maybe I'll see you there," he teased her.

Honor laughed as she continued toward the house. She paused when she reached the doorway and looked back at them.

"Hey," Seth spoke nervously, unsure how to approach his brother. Will turned around and looked at him. He then glanced over his brother's shoulder. Jo had joined Honor outside, watching them from the porch.

Will took a deep breath as he looked back at Seth. "Well, are you going to help or what?" he asked as he handed him a box. Seth nodded as he took the box from his brother and smiled.

~~~

Honor positioned her mother's old chair toward the window. She wanted to be able to look out at the willow tree she had grown fond of as her mother did. Her new room was now complete, with her books now neatly placed on her bookshelf, and her clothes folded in her dresser. She collapsed onto the chair and picked up her new book that Jo had given her.

"Hey," Will said as he stepped into her room. "It's late. You should be in bed."

"Okay, in a minute," she replied from behind her book.

Will walked over and pulled the book from her hands. "I said, to bed," he gave her a warning look.

"Just a few chapters," she pleaded with him.

"No. We've got church in the morning." He set the book onto the shelf. She leaped up out of the chair.

"I'll get up in time," she said as she furtively tried to retrieve the book from the shelf.

"I said no," he grabbed the book before she could pick it up, and hid it behind his back. "Am I going to have to ground you from your books too?"

"You wouldn't do that," she giggled as she playfully tried to snatch the book away from behind him. He grinned and held it over her head.

"Dad, come on. Grandma gave that to me." She jumped up and pulled on his strong arms, trying to get the book, as he flexed his muscles and he teased her, switching it from one hand to the other.

"Maybe I'll just give it back to her then."

"No, I just started reading it," she continued to wrestle with him for the book.

"Give up, you're not going to win," he laughed.

Honor sighed. "Fine," she said as she hugged him. "I'll go to bed."

He let his arms down and hugged her back, letting the book rest on her back. She smiled as she let him go and grabbed the book.

"Just one chapter," she said as she jumped onto her bed.

He shook his head and smiled in amazement of her trickery. "Fine," he put his hands on his hips. "One chapter, then lights out." He walked over to her and sat on the edge of the bed. She slipped under the sheets as he kissed her on her forehead. "I mean it. Just one chapter..."

"I know, I know," she said as she opened the book.

"Goodnight," he kissed her head again as he stood up and walked to the door.

"Dad?"

"Yes," he turned around.

"I love you," she smiled.

"Love you too," he smiled back. "Goodnight."

~~~

Will walked outside as he opened a bottle of beer. He was startled for a moment when his eyes adjusted to the darkness and saw Seth, sitting at the other end of the unlit porch. Though the two men unloaded the truck and trailer together, with the exception of the occasionally grunt at one another about where to put stuff. Neither one of them really spoke a word to each other.

Will met his brother's eyes and nodded at him.

"Thank you for your help today," he said taking a sip of his beer.

"No problem," Seth responded quietly, he too was drinking a beer as he stared out in the darkness.

Will stared off into the distance, unsure what to say to his brother. He was unsure how to break the awkward silence that had wedged between them for so many years. He glanced over at Seth, making eye contact with him.

"Are you still doing your photography stuff?" Will asked quietly.

"Yeah," Seth answered. "You still doing construction?"

"Trying too," Will said as he took another drink of his beer and stared off in the distance. The silence took over again as the two men sipped on their beers as if putting a bottle in front of their lips was excuse not to talk. Seth sighed and cleared his throat. Then he spoke.

"Remember that one time when dad let us camp out under the tree and it was down pouring - ?"

"Let us?" Will interrupted him. "He didn't let us, he made us. He locked us out. Said we couldn't come back in until we stopped fighting."

"Yeah well, whatever the reason. It was fun. Remember mom had a cow because you broke a bunch of branches off the tree to make a shelter." Seth took a sip of his beer. He looked at his brother. Will smiled a little as he looked out at the tree.

"What happen to us? Even though we fought, we were still so close."

"You know why," Will shook his head.

"No, I don't know. Even before Becca. Will, you hated me before she died."

"I hated you because you broke Dads heart, the way you ran off doing whatever with that ... that Tommy Blair kid. Whatever happened to him anyway?"

"Prison."

Will laughed, "See, I could have told you that-that's where he'd end up. A matter of fact I do believe that I did tell you that. You're damn lucky he didn't drag you there with him."

"He wasn't that bad."

"Wasn't that bad, Seth, he made you change your mind about joining the service. You and I were going to serve together, just like dad." Will's voice began to get louder. "Remember? But instead you hung around here with Tommy getting high and whatever else."

"I didn't want to be in the service. That was Dad's plan. And your plan. Not mine. And it's not like you stayed in the service that long anyway, so don't get all high and mighty on me about it."

"Let's not forget that you are the reason why I didn't stay long."

"No, it wasn't me, you couldn't handle it. Becca couldn't handle it either, the way you changed after your tours. You were different when you came home." He walked over to Will.

"Shut up, you don't get to speak for her!" Will yelled.

"Why not? It wasn't like you let her speak for herself when she was alive," Seth snapped. "You were waiting for a reason to quit." Seth stepped closer to Will, he poked him in the chest with his index finger, "And when she died, you took the easy way out. Using her as an excuse."

"Don't!" Will warned his brother.

"And let's not forget what happened after Annie left you the first time." Seth poked him again. "Or did you forget?"

Will pushed Seth back, "Don't!"

"No Will, let's just get this out right now. You'd be dead if I hadn't..."

Will punched him in the mouth before he could finish. And without hesitation, Seth punched him back, hitting him below his right eye. Both men wrestled, falling off the steps onto the ground.

Seth pinned Will to the ground, holding his shoulders down with his hands. "So much for your training, you've gone soft," he antagonized him.

Will quickly lifted his arms between Seth's and above his head. He then twisted his hips; freeing his right leg from beneath his brother then whipped it around him knocking him to the ground as he grabbed his arm and pinning Seth in a leg lock.

"Boys!" Jo yelled, marching out onto the porch. "William, you let your brother up right now."

Will took a deep breath and pushed Seth way from him. They both stood up and brushed themselves off.

"How dare you boys fight like this, your father would be rolling in his grave. Sethaniel get yourself inside and get that lip cleaned up."

Seth spit blood on the ground toward Will feet. "At least you didn't break my jaw this time," he said, glaring at Will as he walked up the steps.

Jo stopped him before he reached the door and took a better look at his mouth. "You better ice that after you clean up."

"Yeah-yeah." Seth responded as he continued to go inside the house.

Will stood still with his arms crossed, staring at the ground.

"And you," she pointed at him. "I expected better from you. Your brother is one thing but you know better."

"Mom, don't."

"I'm not going to stand around and watch you two go at it anymore. You need to resolve this ... this whatever it is between you two and act like brothers again," she said sternly with her hands on her hips. "I was expecting you to be the bigger man. Now if you'll excuse me, I'm going to bed."

CHAPTER 9

Honor and Jo were busy preparing cheesy potatoes and ham in a Crock-Pot for the potluck after church. Honor was cutting the ham into cubes and tossing them into the Crock-Pot and tossing some of the smaller pieces of ham to Finn, who sat patiently behind her between every bite.

"Make sure that some of that ham gets into the casserole and not all on the floor," Jo teased her.

"Morning," Will said as walked into the kitchen and poured himself a cup of coffee.

"Dad, your eye!" Honor exclaimed as she stared at him.

"It's nothing," Will sat down at the table. "What are you two making?"

"Cheesy potatoes with ham," Honor smiled as she walked over to her father and handed him a piece of ham. She gently poked the bruise that had formed under his eye.

"Does it hurt?"

"No," he smiled as he pulled her on his lap. "But you should see the other guy." He hugged her and kissed the top of her head.

"I did see the other guy," she laughed. "Uncle Seth has a fat lip."

"Yeah, what do you know about it?" He hugged her tighter.

"Grandma told me," she laughed as she jumped up from his bear hug. She grabbed a pair of boxing gloves from a box that sat on the counter.

"Here, Grandma found them," she said, tossing them to him.

"Next time you might want to use'em," Jo warned him shaking a wooden spoon at him.

"Mom, I can't believe you still have these," he said as he put them on over his hands.

"Well, I figured you'd need them. Now if you two decide to act like fools then you can do it like your father taught you. Then you can learn how to forgive in church." Jo looked at the clock on the wall, "Speaking of, we're going to be late. Honor, honey, I'll finish here. Why don't you go and get ready for church."

"Okay, come on Finn," Honor called for Finn.

Will waited for her to leave the room. "So, how much did you actually tell her?"

"Just that you two had an argument and that it is over. It's over, right?"

"It depends. Is he gone?"

"William, you know I wish you could just forgive and forget the past. Your brother is a different man now."

"Well he was the same old jerk last night," Will smirked. "Mom, I can't stand him."

"He's cleaned up his act and wants nothing more than you to accept him for who he is."

"Did he say that? Or are you speaking for him?"

Jo sat down at the table, "He's changed. You've changed. Just talk with him and keep your fists out of it. You'll see that there is no reason for this anger between you two to go on anymore," She pleaded with him as she reached out and held his hand. "It hurts me so much that my boys hate each other."

He could see in her eyes that this brotherly feud was breaking her heart.

"I'm sorry, mom. I can't promise you anything except that I'll try my best not to hit him again."

"William," Jo slapped his arm and gave him a stern look.

Will grinned, "Okay, I'll try talking to him."

"That's all I ask," She smiled.

~~~

Honor walked into the fellowship hall of the small church, with her grandmother's Crock-Pot in hand. She needed to find somewhere to plug it in so that the casserole could continue to cook during church service. A woman, dressed in her Sunday's best, smiled at Honor as she set down a plastic covered, plate of brownies and left the room.

Honor walked over to the long table along the wall. One end of the table had an assortment of desserts like cookies, pie, cake, brownies, and something strange covered in powdered sugar. On the other end there were Crock-Pots, lots of Crock-Pots. Honor carefully placed hers on the table. She followed the other cords with her eyes that led her to beneath the table where two power strips laid on the floor. She placed her cord between the wall and the table, like the others, then she crawled under the table and plugged hers in an empty socket on the power strip.

Curiously, she peeked in the lids of some of the other Crock-Pots. "Wow, that a lot of Mac 'n' cheese," she said to herself out loud, as she discovered that at least five of the Crock-Pots were simmering with the familiar side dish.

~~~

The congregation were on their feet and singing the opening hymn when Honor joined her father and grandmother four rows from the back of the sanctuary. She nudged her father and smiled. He smiled through his singing and nudged her back gently.

The sanctuary was small and was filled row to row with people. Most of them were dressed in their Sunday's best and others casual. The choir stood to the right of the pulpit and were wearing blue and white robes. A large cross hung high behind the pulpit.

Honor giggled as she heard her father's voice crack a few times as he sang. Will ignored her as his attention was drawn toward the other end of the pew.

Seth walked in and excused himself through the row of people. He was dressed nicely with jeans and a tie. His lip was still swollen. He avoided eye contact with his brother hiding behind his sunglasses. He sat down in the empty space next to Jo.

A woman in the row in front of them recognized the McFadden brothers behind her. She looked at Seth and his lip then at Will and his eye. Will smiled at her and acknowledged her with a slight nodded. She turned around and faced forward. There were a few other people who were baffled as well when they had notice the estranged brothers in the same pew, some more discreetly than others.

When the song was over, everyone sat down. Pastor Brock stood up from the front pew and walked up to the pulpit.

"Good morning." He greeted the congregation. "I just have a few announcements. The Ladies Friendship will be meeting in the fellowship hall next Tuesday instead of Thursday. This will be a potluck lunch. Men's Breakfast on Saturday morning will be meeting at the diner, instead of here." Pastor Brock cleared his throat, "Now it's my pleasure to announce that we have a special singer with us today. Emily, Jan and Gary's granddaughter is here. It's a great Blessing for us to have her again to sing for us. Please help me welcome Emily as she sings Amazing Grace."

The congregation applauded. Honor watched in awe as Emily, a young blind girl walked up to the microphone. As the piano began playing, Emily took a breath then began to sing. Her beautiful voice gave Honor chills.

~~~

After the service Will sat down at the table near the back of the fellowship hall. Honor and Jo were getting drinks as Jo introduced her granddaughter to some of the ladies. Honor smiled awkwardly at her father as the eldest lady, Mrs. Redman, pinched her cheeks. Will chuckled and shook his head as he took a bite of his mac 'n' cheese. He was glad that he was able make it safely to the table without getting cornered by Mrs. Redman.

Honor walked quickly over to her father, the moment she could politely break away from the cheek pincher. She handed him one of the glasses of water and sat down in front of her plate.

"I see you met Mrs. Redman," Will grinned.

Honor rubbed her cheeks, "For an old lady, she has quite a grip. I thought she was going to pinch my face off."

"Is that all you are eating?" he asked as he pointed to her plate, it held only a small scoop of Jo's ham and potato casserole and a pile of pickles.

"There's nothing but macaroni and cheese. I should have brought one of your MRE's. At least there were pickles," Honor said as she bit into one of the pickles from her plate.

Jo walked over and sat down next to Will.

"I just can't get over how great Mrs. Redman looks. Did you know she just turned eight-seven? And she still drives herself to church."

"I've heard she has quite the grip too," Will teased, looking over at Honor.

"She still lives in that old house down on second street and she told me that she needs someone to patch a hole in the roof. It started leaking after the storm we just had. So I told her that I'd send you her way after you were done eating."

"Just don't let her get a hold of your face," Honor grinned as she stuffed another pickle in her mouth. Will stared at his daughter and smiled as he shook his head.

"William," Pastor Brock greeted him as he approached their table. "I am so glad that you are here."

Will stood from his chair and shook Brock's hand, "Thank you. It was a beautiful service."

"Thank you. You must be Honor." Brock turned toward her with a smile. "Your Grandmother has told me so much about you."

"Good things, I hope," Honor giggled as she stuffed another pickle in her mouth.

"Yes, all good things. So William you are quite the buzz around town. Folks are saying you are going to be our new handyman."

"Ahh, yeah. I guess so," Will said as he looked at Jo with a puzzled look on his face. "But I'm not sure how it got out so fast."

"Well you know in a small town like ours, word travels fast."

"Yeah, I guess it does."

"Speaking of, I thought I saw your brother sitting with you. Is he still here?"

"He was but you know Seth, he's not very social."

"Well maybe I'll catch up with him some other time. It was good to see you two in the same room."

"Yeah, I think we confused a few people."

"They're just curious. It's been a long time." Brock smiled, "I hope that things are going well between you two."

"Dad gave Uncle Seth a fat lip," Honor blurted out as she shuffled a bite of her casserole in her mouth.

"Honor," Will shook his head at her. "We had a disagreement that's all," He turned to Brock. "We're working on it," Will smiled at Jo, then at Brock.

"Well my door is always open if you need anything," Brock smiled.

"Thank you."

CHAPTER 10

Finn perked his head up when Seth walked into the house and into the living room. Seth looked at the lazy dog.

"Better not let Jo see you sitting on her couch," he said to Finn as the dog laid his head back down.

Seth shook his head and hung his jacket on the back of the recliner. He loosened his tie and collar as he walked up the stairs to change his clothes.

Shortly behind him Jo and Will came in the front door. Finn jumped off from the couch and laid on the floor when he heard them come in the house.

Jo sighed, "What a day?"

"Mom, are you okay?" Will asked as he took the empty Crock-Pot from her.

"Yes dear," she assured him. "Sundays just wear me out, especially potluck Sundays. I think I'll go lie down for a bit."

"Okay," He said as she walked up the stairs. He noticed Finn lying on the floor.

"Good boy, fuss."

Will took the Crock-Pot to the kitchen and placed it on the counter. Finn followed close to his heels and nudged the back of Will's thigh with his nose.

"Okay boy," Will turned around to Finn. "Need to go outside?" Finn jumped and paced back and forth from Will and the front door as Will walked back to the living room toward the door. Finn's rear end bumped the back of the recliner where Seth's jacket was, knocking the jacket onto the floor. "Calm down boy," Will warned the dog as he opened the door. Finn ran outside.

Will stood in the doorway for a moment and watched Finn dash around the yard with his nose to the ground.

He turned and noticed that Seth's jacket was on the floor. As he picked it up and flung it back on the recliner a small baggie fell from one of the pockets. Will picked up the clear baggie, which contained five rolled joints in it.

Will's face turn red with anger. "I'm going to kill him," he said to himself as he marched up the stairs and into Seth's room.

Seth was changing his shirt when Will walked into the room.

"What the hell is this?" Will demanded loudly, as he tossed the baggie of joints at his brother.

"What? You're going through my pockets now?" Seth glared at Will.

"No! It fell from your jacket. How dare you bring this into the house that my twelve year old daughter is in?" Will yelled.

"Will, it's not mine."

"Oh yeah, then just who does it belong to and why was it in your jacket?"

"It's mine, William," Jo entered the room. Will turned around as Jo walked toward Seth. Seth handed the baggie to her.

"What?" Will looked at Jo.

"I told Sethaniel to keep it between us but I guess the cat is out of the bag now," Jo said as she took a deep breath and sat down on the bed.

"So what? You're smoking pot now?" Will looked at her sternly as he crossed his arm.

"William, don't look at me like that. Sit down," she said sadly as she pat the bed next to her.

Will's face softened, "Mom, what's going on?"

"Sit and I'll tell you."

Will looked at his brother as he sat down next to Jo. Seth leaned against the wall with a blank expression on his face as he stared at the floor.

"Several months ago, I had gone to the doctors due to headaches that I had thought to be migraines. They ran some tests and found out that they were not migraines and that I had a tumor on my brain." Jo took Will's hand, "I have cancer, William."

"Mom," Will eyes swelled. "How bad is it? What's the treatment plan?"

"There is none? I have decided that instead of wasting away in the hospital and being sick from chemo and radiation that being at home is where I belong. And being here was the best place to spend whatever time I have left."

"There's got to be more options. What about surgery?"

"It's inoperable," Seth spoke up.

"So how long have you known?" Will snapped at his brother. Seth gave Will a quick, angry glare.

"Now don't get upset at him. He didn't find out until I requested him to get me this."

"So you're just going to get high and give up? Mom, you can't give up. What about Honor? What about us?"

"I'm not giving up," Jo reached out for Seth's hand. Seth held her hand but continued to look blankly at the floor. "Giving up is not living life to the fullest. And right now I'm happy with my decision. I have everything I want here. Honor and you two all under the same roof."

"That's why you pushed me so hard to move in here, wasn't it?" Will stood up. "Did you think I'd move in and just take care of you until you died?"

"No, now that was not my intentions. My wish was to leave the house to you and Honor and with you already living here, it makes it easier for the transitions. And when the time comes, Pastor Brock will take me to Hospice. I have made him power of attorney."

"I need some air," Seth said as he walked quickly out of the room.

"Seth!" Will tried to stop him.

"William," Jo pulled him back to her. "Just let him go."

Will took a deep breath, "Are you sure this is what you want?"

"Yes. This is what I want. And I want your full support on this."

"Okay. Okay."

Jo hugged Will and kissed him on the cheek. "It's going to be fine. I promise."

"What about Honor? What do you want me to tell her?" Will asked.

"I could hardly tell you boys. I can't even imagine how I could tell her."

"Mom, I can't keep this from her."

"I know and you shouldn't. You can tell her when you think the time is right."

"Okay."

"It's going to be okay," she hugged him again. "Now if you don't mind, I'm going to go and finish my nap." Jo smiled, "We'll talk some more later." She stood from the bed and walked out of room, leaving Will still sitting on the bed.

Jo walked to her bedroom and closed the door. She placed the baggie of joints in her top dresser drawer then sat down on her bed. Tears that she had held back from her sons, streamed down her cheek. She laid down on her bed and closed her eyes.

~~~

"How about this one?" Annie asked as she held up a pink dress with roses laced around the hips.

Honor scrunched up her nose and shook her head, "Lame, too pink."

"Okay," Annie skimmed through the rack of dresses. "What colors do you like?"

"Black." Honor pulled a black dress from the rack, "How about this?" She held the dress up for Annie to see.

"Maybe... if we were going to a funeral," Annie smiled.

Honor sighed, "Maybe I should just wear jeans. I've never really been good at dressing up."

"Your dad never took you dress shopping?"

"Have you met my dad? He's not what you call a classy dresser. Cargo pants and a t-shirt is what he calls formal wear."

"Point taken," Annie laughed. "Okay, how about this one?" She held out a dark purple dress that was slim and flared out at the bottom.

Honor smiled and nodded her head.

"Why don't you go and try this on," Annie handed her the dress.

Honor walked into the fitting room and closed the door. Annie sat down in a chair next to the room.

"Annie?" Honor asked through the door.

"Yeah?"

"Are you and my dad dating? Or just...uh, you know...?"

"Oh uh, you know your dad and I are good friends and we've known each other a long time."

"So you two are just friends?" Honor asked despondently as she pulled the dress on and admired herself in the mirror.

"You sound disappointed."

"Well. Don't tell him that I said this, but I really think he needs to put himself out there. He's been alone for so long that..." Honor sighed. "I really was hoping that maybe you and he would ... could be together," Honor poked her head out of the door of the dressing room.

"Well don't tell him I told you this. Your dad and I have been talking about that and we decided to take it slow. So who knows," Annie smiled.

Honor smiled back as she walked out of the doorway.

"Wow, it is perfect. What do you think? Do you like it?"

"I love it," Honor smiled in the mirror twisting around to view the dress from the back.

Annie pulled out her cell phone, "Should we take a picture and send it to your dad?"

"No. I think we should surprise him," Honor said as she twirled in front of the triple mirror outside the fitting room.

"Well, he is going to love it," Annie hugged her. "Now, how about shoes?"

Honor smiled, "I know just the pair."

~~~

Seth stood inside the old pole barn; he put his hand on his hips and looked around at all the junk that had accumulated over the years. He tried not to think about his mother. He walked over to a pile of boxes and opened one of them.

"Hey," Will said from behind him.

"What do you want now?" Seth mumbled.

"I think we should talk about this."

"Talk about what?"

"Mom." Will walked over to his brother. "She needs to fight this. We have to convince her to - "

"Convince her to do what? She said there's no treatment. No operation. No options." Seth angrily pushed over the pile of boxes and turned around to face Will. "Don't you get it? She doesn't want to fight it!"

Seth turned back around to hide his tearful eyes from his big brother. He saw the mess he made, "Damn it." He knelt down and picked up the photographs that he spilled from the boxes.

"Seth," Will approached him and put his hand on his shoulder. Seth sniffled as he moved from his brother's hand.

"Remember this," Seth lifted a photo of himself and Will when they were kids, young images of the men they were today, except then they were happy together. "Look how scrawny you use to be."

"I wouldn't be talking you were the smallest one in your class," Will teased him as he knelt down next to Seth, helping him pick up the photographs. "Here, look at this one."

"Oh my God is that dad?" Seth looked closer at the photo. "I don't remember dad dressing up like Santa."

"Because you cried that year, you had nightmares about dad in a scary red suit. He never wore it again after that."

"Whatever," Seth continued to shuffle through the other boxes. He found an old photo of himself, Will, Becca and Annie when they were kids. They were all hanging on a branch of the willow tree. "Here, maybe you should give this one to Honor."

"Wow, I didn't think mom kept any of these," Will commented as he flipped through a few of the photos.

"I know it's not my place. But what's up with you and Annie?" Seth looked at his brother with concern.

"What do you mean?"

"Well the last time you two hooked up, I had to pick up all the broken pieces of your heart she had ripped out."

"It's different this time, and you're right it's not your place," Will said quickly as he turned his focus to the back wall of the barn.

Seth took deep breath. "I just wanted to know whether or not to wear a vest around you."

Will looked at his brother. "Don't worry. I haven't carried my sidearm since I've been here," Will snickered. "Hey what's this?" Will changed the subject as he quickly pulled a canvas tarp off from a half built wooden bench. Seth coughed as he waved his hands in the air swaying the dust from his face.

"This must of been the project dad was working on before his stroke."

"By the looks of it he was almost done," Seth admired the wooden bench. "All it needs is some lacquer. Tighten a few screws." Seth stepped back for a moment and stared at it. He looked back at the box of old photographs and smiled. "Yeah, I've got it."

"Got what?"

"I'm going to finish it for mom," Seth said confidently. "Maybe not quite what dad wanted but I think she is going to love it."

CHAPTER 11

Annie and Honor had pulled into the driveway, when Will walked out onto the porch. Annie smiled when her eyes met his. Honor noticed the look between them and giggled.

"See. I told you that you make him happy."

"Well, the feeling is mutual," Annie nudge Honor's shoulder. "Now don't tell him about any our conversations. What's said between girls stays between girls."

"I won't. Thank you for taking me shopping. It was fun," Honor said as she open the passenger's side door.

"Your welcome. I had fun too."

"I'll see you later," Honor waved at Annie as she jumped out of the car and ran toward the house with her shopping bag.

"Hi dad. Bye dad," she said to him as she tried to run past him.

"Hey, aren't you forgetting something?" he stepped in front of her.

She stopped and hugged him. "Sorry, Love you," she said with excitement as she continued toward the house.

"Hey, what's your rush?"

"I want to show Grandma Jo my new dress!" Honor stopped on the porch swinging the shopping bag around.

"Well that'll have to wait, she's resting. So don't wake her up. Just go put it in your room for now. And come back down," He instructed her.

"Okay," Honor sighed as she walked into the house with disappointment.

Will shook his head and smiled as he made his way over to Annie's car. Annie turned the engine off. Will leaned into her window, resting his arms on the window seal.

"Hi," He smiled as he leaned in closer to kiss her. She met him halfway and greeted his lips with hers.

"Hi yourself," She smiled through the kiss.

"So did you two have fun?"

"Yes, yes we did."

"What did you ladies talk about?"

Annie giggled, "It's classified. And I'm afraid that you don't have gal-clearance."

"Gal-clearance?" he laughed. "Clever."

"I thought so," she grinned.

"So uh, do you want to come in for awhile?"

"I'd love too, but I should really get back to the house. Knowing Val, she is going to want to go over the final plans for the week."

"Yeah, okay." Will looked back at the house.

"You okay?" Annie asked.

"Yeah. I'm fine," he sighed.

"Are you sure? Cause you have that confused look again, like you need to say something but you just don't know how to start."

"Uh you know me a little too well. You know that don't you."

"Will, whatever it is you can tell me."

"Yeah, I know," Will looked at Annie's cell phone as it began to ring.

"I'm sorry," she silenced the phone when she saw that it was her sister calling.

"Your sister?"

"Yes," Annie stared at her phone as it rang again. "I'm sorry. I better go."

"No. It's okay. We'll catch up later."

"Are you sure?"

"Yeah. Call me later when your sister is done with you," he grinned.

"Oh, I will," she smiled as she started the engine. Will leaned in the window and kissed her goodbye.

Honor walked out of the house as Annie drove away. Will walked over to her.

"How about you and I get some ice cream?" Will offered.

"That sounds like an excellent idea," Honor grinned. "I'll get your keys." She ran inside and grabbed her father's keys from the small bowl sitting on the table next to the door.

Will whistled, "Finn! Here boy!" He whistled again as he let down the tailgate. Finn came running from around the house and leaped into the bed of the truck.

Honor ran out from the house, she tossed her father his keys.

"Ready?" Will open her door for her.

"Yep!" She hopped into the truck.

~~~

Finn wagged his tail wildly. He paced in the back of the truck as Honor and Will walked out of the ice cream shop.

"Finn, platz," Will commanded him. Finn laid down as Will let down the tailgate and sat down on it.

Honor licked her ice cream cone as she hopped up onto the gate next to her father.

"Do you think you and Annie will get married?" Honor asked between licks.

Will nearly choked on his ice cream. "Uh, what?"

"Dad, don't be so dramatic. It's just a question."

"How's your ice cream?" Will took a big bite off of his cone. "Mine's fantastic." He continued with his mouth full. A little bit of melted chocolate drooled from his mouth. He grinned at her with the mess on his chin. Honor looked at him and then looked at a woman who was walking by. Will made eye contact with the woman and he quickly wiped his mouth off with his napkin.

"You're embarrassing," Honor laughed at him. "And you are evading my questions again."

"Baby, Annie and I just started to seeing each other. Marriage is not on our minds right now."

"Why not?"

"Because it's not."

"But you love her right?" Honor stared at him. "And you two did stay the night together," she hinted.

"I don't like the way this is going," he avoided his daughter's eye contact.

"I've seen the way you look at her. The way you kiss her," she teased him.

"When have you seen me kiss her?"

"Uh, today when she dropped me off."

"You were supposed to be in the house."

"I was in the house, there's things called windows. You can see out of them."

"Well, you weren't supposed to be spying on us."

"Well, I couldn't help it. Grandma has all the curtains pulled wide open all the time."

Will thought about Jo. He knew he had to tell his daughter. The very thought of her losing her grandmother so soon, gave him chills. Will leaped off of the tailgate. "You ready to go?" he asked as he stuffed the last part of his cone in his mouth.

"Where are we going?" she asked as she too jumped from the back of the truck.

"Somewhere I should have taken you when we first got here."
Honor gave Finn the last bite of her cone.
"Hey, you know that's not good for him." Will said as he put the
tailgate upright. "I've never known you to throw away ice cream."
"It's just vanilla. Besides I had ice cream with Annie earlier."
"Really?"
Honor grinned and nodded her head as they both got into the truck
and drove down the street.

~~~

They pulled onto a long gravel road that curved through a wooded
area. A short iron fence lined a small cemetery.
"Is this where mom is?" Honor asked as she stared at the iron
archway. Will nodded as he stopped the truck in the grassy area outside the
fence.
"Come on." Will turned off the ignition and stepped out of the truck.
Honor got out and walked to the archway as Will opened the tailgate for
Finn. The dog jumped out and ran over to Honor. She waited for her father
to join her. Will put his arm around her shoulder as the two of them walked
into the cemetery with Finn behind them.
"It's beautiful here," Honor said as she took in the view. She looked
ahead curiously, studying each headstone. "Which one is it?"
Will pointed at the large willow tree next to the back of the fence,
"There."
"She's under the willow?" Honor asked. "It looks just like the one at
home."
"Well it should. I planted it from one of the branches off of the tree at
home."
"For mom?"
"I told you she loved that tree. I wanted a part of it to be with her
always. And by the look of it, it has grown."
Honor stopped at the head stone that lay just beneath the tips of the
branches. She knelt down next to it and read it.

<div align="center">

Rebecca Lynn McFadden
July 11th, 1979
August 26th, 2003
Wife, Mother and Friend

</div>

"Do you think that mom is really watching over us from heaven?"
"I don't know. Maybe she just checks in on us from time to time."

"Annie told me she had some videos of you guys when you were my age. She said she'd bring them over when she finds them."

"That's nice of her."

"Do you think mom would be okay that you are dating her best friend?"

"I think she knows that no one can ever replace her and the timing of which God placed Annie back in my life is okay with her."

"And the timing of God bringing you and Uncle Seth back together. So you two could forgive each other."

"Yes. I suppose so."

"And the timing of me getting into a fight with Amber and you losing your job, so that we could get some time off to come here?"

"Yeah. I guess the chain of events brought us where we are today," Will smiled, "and thank you."

"For what?"

"For reminding me that you are still grounded," Will grinned. "I think Grandma has a few toilets to clean when we get home."

~~~

Will stopped the truck at the edge of the driveway and put it into park with the engine still running.

"Why'd you stop?" Honor asked. She noticed the blank stare on his face as he looked forward, toward the house. "Dad?"

Will turned to her. "Honor, sweetheart. I need to tell you something. Something about Jo."

He cleared his throat when he saw the complete attention she gave him. "Your grandma is..." He choked back his tears by taking another breath. "Well, baby she's sick."

"I don't understand. She seemed fine this morning."

"I know. She, uh ... she has tumor in her brain. And there's not much that the doctors can do to help her get better."

"Can't the doctors remove it?" she asked as a tear rolled down her cheek.

Will shook his head.

"So, she's going to die?" Honor cried.

Will nodded. Tears rolled down his face as he drew Honor closer to him. She buried her head into his chest.

"How long does she have?" She sniffled as she looked up at him.

"I don't know, baby. I don't know." He kissed her on the top off her head as he hugged her tightly as she wept.

CHAPTER 12

"Lemonade, William?" asked a sweet elderly voice.

Will peered over the edge of the roof to see Mrs. Redman holding a tray of cookies and a glass of lemonade.

"Thank you, Mrs. Redman. Maybe in a bit," Will answered her as he continued to hammer.

"I said. Do you want some lemonade?" she repeated louder.

Will put the hammer down. "Yes, mama. I'll be down later. Thank you," he said louder.

Mrs. Redman kept looking up at him with a puzzled look on her face. "Dear, I don't have the slightest idea where your ladder is," she shouted as she began looking around the house for the ladder.

Will shook his head and put his tools aside. His mother had warned him that, Mrs. Redman forgets to put her hearing aides in. Today is one of those days that she forgot to put them in and yelling from the roof would probably just confuse her more. He steadily walked across the roof to where the ladder was and climbed down. Mrs. Redman was still looking up at the roof when Will walked over to her. She turned around.

"Oh good. You found the ladder," she smiled as she set the tray down on the patio table and handed him the glass of lemonade.

"Thank you, ma'am." He said loud enough so she could hear him this time.

"You're welcome dear. I'm just so glad to have a handsome young man to come over and help me." She reached out with her hand toward his cheek. Awkwardly, he gently welcomed her hand into his, converting her cheek pinch into a handshake.

"Well, drink your lemonade dear. Can't have you dehydrated on a count of me," she smiled, letting go of his hand. "It was just dreadful the way the shingles blew right off from the storm," she said as she walked back toward the house.

Will shook his head as he watched the deaf elderly woman talk to herself as she went inside. He set down his glass on the table and snagged a cookie. He stuffed it into his mouth as he climbed back onto the ladder. He had just picked up his hammer when his phone rang. It was Annie calling.

"I was wondering when you were going to call me," he answered his phone. He smiled as he sat down on the roof, "Tonight? Yeah, I could probably get away." He paused. The sound of her voice made him grin ear to ear.

"I'll pick you up at six then," he agreed. "Okay, see you tonight, bye." He sighed with excitement as he put his phone in his pocket and continued fixing the roof.

~~~

Honor stepped into the pole barn. Seth was finishing last coat of lacquer on the bench. She plugged her nose as she walked up from behind him.

"Uncle Seth," she said her voice altered due to her plugged nose.

Seth turned around, "Hey girl. What'cha up to?"

"Nothing." She saw his eyes peering at her above the bandana that covered his nose and mouth. "You look like a bank robber from the old west." She giggled as she unplugged her nose.

"Oh yeah, maybe I was one in a past life."

"I don't think so. You can only have one life."

Seth set his brush down sideways on top of the can of finish.

"Are you finished?" Honor asked as she admired the bench.

"I think so, just have to let this coat dry," he stepped back and wiped his hands off on a rag. He looked at her curiously. "You know I think this is the first time I've seen you without a book."

"Just taking a break," she smiled as she pulled a picture from a nearby box. The picture was of her mother when she was young.

"Did you know her very well, you know when she was older?"

"Sure. Your mom and I hung out from time to time, while your dad was deployed."

"Really?"

"Yeah. I kinda helped her out around the house when she was pregnant with you."

"So you guys must have talked a lot."

"I wouldn't really say we talked a lot. But yeah we talked. She mainly spoke about how excited she was to bring you into the world. Your mom was an incredible woman. She'd be proud of the an amazing young lady you've become."

Seth looked at Honor, then down at the floor.

"You took the pictures of them. The ones on grandma's walls."

"Yeah. I took those before your dad was deployed. Your mom wanted your dad to have some good pictures to take with him."

Honor saw the glossy look in her uncle's eyes when he said the part about her mother.

"It's not your fault you know," Honor said quietly. "I know that dad blamed you for along time. But it wasn't your fault."

"Thank you."

"You're welcome," Honor smiled as she climbed up on a hay bail. She sat with her knees to her chest. She then pulled the hood from her sweatshirt over her head and slipped the front of her sweatshirt over her knees, creating a cocoon with only her face and the toes of her shoes peering from the sweatshirt.

Seth watched her as she pulled on the drawstrings framing her face with the hood.

"Hey. Stay right there. Just like that," he said as he walked over to the work bench and grabbed his camera. "Do you mind?" he asked as he held his camera up.

Honor smiled as she shook her head. Seth snapped a photo then knelt down to shoot a few more at different angles. He scanned through the photos on his viewfinder.

"Awesome. Now how about a scary one." He put the camera back up to his face.

"Like this?" she asked as she gnashed her teeth at him from the shadows of her hood.

"Yeah girl, perfect. Just keep making faces at me," he said as he continued shooting.

"Uncle Seth?" Honor flipped her hood off from her head.

"Yeah?" he answered as he looked down at the photos on the viewfinder.

"Can you teach me how to use your camera? And take pictures like the ones in your portfolio?"

"Yeah-yeah. Of course I can," Seth smiled. "Come-on. I have an idea."

Honor jumped down from the hay bail and followed him outside.

~~~

Will picked Annie up at six o'clock. They ate dinner at the diner, where they talked about the good old days. Will shared with her about his mother.

They then drove across town to play miniature golf. Will enjoyed every minute with Annie. She distracted him from thinking about his mother and his financial problems. He felt alive and happy again.

Annie placed her purple golf ball onto the green. She was well aware of Will standing behind her as she bent over knowing he would check out her behind.

"Are you trying to flirt with me?" he asked as he walked up behind her. He placed his hands on her hips as she stood up straight.

"Why whatever gave you that impression?" she smiled, looking at him over her shoulder. She gripped the putter in her hands and nudged him back with her behind as she lined herself up with the ball. His hands glided from her hips to her arms as he stepped in closer from behind her. Placing his hands next to hers on the putter. She giggles as she pulls the putter back lightly to take a swing. He sways along with her and just before she hit the ball, he kisses her neck. She missed the ball completely and she turned around to look at him.

"You made me miss!" she said.

"I did not," he grinned as he pulled his ball from his pocket and placed it on the green. "And that did count as a stroke," he teased her.

"Oh. So that's how we are going to play this?" she laughed.

"I don't know what you're talking about. It's not my fault that you can't concentrate on something so simple like playing mini golf," he teased her as he set up his shot.

She giggled and bit her bottom lip as she wrapped her arms around his waist. He shook his head and smiled as he pulled the putter back. She then slid her hands from his abs and into the front pockets of his blue jeans as he swung. He jerked forward as he hit the ball, sending it off of the green and into the rocks.

"I think that counts as two strokes," she laughed as she backed up and marked his stoke down on their scorecard.

He walked up to her and snagged the scorecard playfully away from her. "We don't need to keep score," he said as he tossed it up in the air behind him as he grabbed her and wrapped her up in his arms. He kissed her.

"So I win?" she asked.

"Yeah," he kissed her again. "You win."

~~~

Will laid some of his clothes out on the bed. It has been a long time since he had to dress up. His first choice was a pair of black slacks that he had not worn in years. He examined them and noticed that were faded, and that was unacceptable.

He tossed them aside and grabbed a pair of his cargo pants. He laid them out on the bed. He stared at them for a moment and shrugged his shoulders. He then shuffled through his closet for a shirt. He selected three of his best and begun placing them one by one on top of the cargo pants to see which one looked best. He decided on his black, long sleeve, button down. He stood back and looked at the outfit he put together.

"You aren't planning on wearing that to the wedding? Are you?" Seth asked as he entered the room.

"What's wrong with it?"

Seth laughed, "What's wrong with it? Are you serious? You can't go to a wedding wearing that."

"Why not?"

"Because you can't," Seth walked over to the closet and begun to sift through Will's clothes. "This is all you got? What's with all the cargo pants?"

Will shrugged his shoulders.

"Look, I know it's been awhile since you've dated. But this whole rugged, working man look will not fly when your date is going to dress to impress."

"What?"

"Okay," Seth sighed. "She sees you in this, all the time. This is what she will expect." He pointed at Will outfit. "You've got to step it up, bro. Don't you have a suit or something?"

"No."

"Well, you can't wear that. You should go buy a suit or at least rent a tux. You don't want your twelve year old daughter to out dress you, do you?"

"Honor showed you her dress?"

"Yes. And she made me pinky swear not to tell you anything about it."

"I bet she did," Will laughed.

The two men stood there for a moment staring at the bed of clothes. Will sighed as he sat on the bed.

"Come on." Seth batted at Will's arm.

"Where are we going?"

"Shopping."

CHAPTER 13

Annie entered the large fitting room with her sister, Valerie. A long beautiful, white wedding dress hung on a hook next to an oversized mirror on the wall.

"Oh Val. It's gorgeous," Annie commented as she admired the fabric on the gown.

"Thank you," Valerie sighed. "Now let's see if it still fits," she said as she undressed down to her under garments.

Annie helped her take the dress down carefully from it's hanger. "I just can't believe that this time tomorrow you'll be married. My little sister married."

"Yeah, we all thought you'd be first. What ever happen with that guy you were dating in Chicago?"

"I caught him cheating on me."

"Annie, I'm so sorry. What happened?" Valerie asked as she unfastened the back of the dress.

"I came home late one night and found him in bed with some other women. So I broke up with him," Annie said sadly as helped her slip the wedding gown over her head. "The funny thing is that I thought Eric was the one."

"At least you have Will now," Valerie assured her sister. "Maybe he is supposed to be the one. I mean you two already have history."

"Well, we're taking it slow. He's being cautious and it's different than before."

"So you guys haven't?"

Annie shook head as she pulled the dress together and began to fasten the buttons on the back of the dress.

"You haven't had sex yet?" Valerie questioned her as she looked at her through the mirror.

84

"No we haven't. He wants to wait and I'm okay with that," Annie smiled. "To tell you the truth, I don't think he has been with anyone since we…"

"What a minute. He hasn't had sex since you two?" Valerie suggested.

"I don't think so." Annie fastened the last clasp on the back of the dress.

"Haven't you two compared war stories about past relationships?" Valerie straightened the fabric in front of her dress and admired herself in the mirror.

"No, I haven't even told him about Eric, yet."

"Okay, let me get this straight. You guys don't talk about sex? You guys don't have sex? What the hell have you two been doing this whole time?"

"We've been getting to know each other again. It's not all about sex. He has this gentle innocence about him when it comes to intimacy. It's hard to describe."

"It's been a long time since you two have been together. Are you sure he's okay down there?"

"Val!"

"What? I'm just saying that maybe you should sample the dessert before you settle down with the main course. And it's super weird that he want to wait. Usually men are the first ones that want to jump in bed."

"Will is different now. He's changed but in a good way."

"Well his brother hasn't," Valerie smiled. "He is still the same handsome gentleman he always was."

"When did you see Seth?" Annie asked.

"He came by the house the other day. He said he wanted to meet Greg. But I really think he was checking him out, you know, just to see what kind of man I was about to marry."

"Why did you invite your ex-boyfriend to your wedding?"

"Seth and I still care about each other. We've talked on the phone over the years. And in a way he's a good friend."

"So you don't have feelings for him anymore?"

"Of course I still have feelings for him. I love him, but I'm just not in love with him. We had our shot. But he wasn't ready to commit. And that's when Greg came into my live. And I just knew that Greg was the one." Valerie smiled at her sister. "You know maybe Eric cheating on you was a sign that you and he were not to be."

"Obviously," Annie noted.

"Yeah okay. But think about it. If he hadn't cheated on you-you wouldn't have come to town as early as you did. And you wouldn't have ran into Will. I mean you would have eventually but not as soon as you did," Valerie smiled again. "He's the one. Fate brought you two together."

Annie smiled back. "I hope so."

"I know so. But I still think it's a little weird that you guys haven't done it yet," Valerie teased her.

"Oh stop it," Annie laughed.

CHAPTER 14

Will straightened his suit as he walked down the stairs. Honors jaw dropped when she saw her father in his dark gray, pinstripe suit, and a silver tie, against his black shirt. His face was freshly shaven and his once long hair, now cut high and tight, military style.

"Dad! Your hair?" Honor gasped.

"Wow son, you look sharp!" Jo commented.

"You're going to be the best looking bachelor there." Honor smiled.

"Thank you, sweetheart. You look amazing as well, look at you!" He took her by the hand and guided her to twirl.

She was in a dark purple, short sleeve dress that flared at the bottom, just below her knees. Her shoes were black converse high tops that were calf high with white laces.

"Those shoe look awesome," he added.

"Annie picked out the dress and I picked out the shoes," she said proudly.

"You are beautiful honey." He wrapped her up in his arms and kissed the top of her head.

Seth walked into the room. He too was all dressed up, his cheeks shaved and his goatee trimmed.

"Uncle Seth look at my dad's hair!"

"I see," he smiled at her. "It's about time you chopped off that mop," Seth said to his brother.

"Yeah, yeah. You clean up nice yourself, if only you could do something about your ugly mug," Will teased him.

"Oh, stop it you two," Jo smiled. "Now, come on, stand together," she ordered them. "I need a picture of this. Seth where's your camera?"

"Here," Seth walked over to his camera bag by the doorway. He pulled his camera out.

"Here give me that," Jo gently snatched it from his hands. "Now get over there with your brother."

"Oh Mom, really?" Seth shook his head. "Do you even know how to use that?"

"Don't you oh Mom me, Sethaniel," she ordered him. "Of course I know how to use this. Who do you think taught you about photography?"

She looked at the camera. She turned it around and around, "Oh dear. How do you turn it on?"

Seth hovered over Jo's shoulder. He smirked as he pushed a button on the camera. The camera beeped and the lens zoomed out, "Okay, okay. I've got it. Now get over there."

Will pulled Seth toward him by the shoulder as Honor stood in front of them and posed for the picture.

The camera flashed. "Okay just one more," she requested as she took a few more pictures.

"Grandma that was more than one," Honor pointed out.

"Okay Mom, we've gotta get going or we'll be late," Will said as he walked over to Jo, giving her a hug.

Seth took his camera from her hand and placed it back into his bag. He then flung the bag over his shoulder as he walked out the door with Will and Honor.

"Have fun." Jo hugged Honor tightly. "Now you keep an eye on these two. Don't let them drink too much at the reception."

"I won't, Grandma. Bye."

~~~

When they arrived, the church was packed with wedding guests. Annie was standing outside the doorway of the sanctuary. She was greeting the guests and handing out wedding programs. Her eyes lit up with surprise when she saw Will and Honor walk into the church.

"Excuse me, could you take these for a minute? I'll be right back," she politely asked another attendant as she handed the programs to them.

"Will, wow you look great!" She greeted him. She brushed the back of his head as they hugged. "And your hair!"

"Thank you. I needed a change. You look amazing," he kissed her lips. Honor giggled. Anne turned toward her.

"And you Honor, wow! You are so beautiful."

"Thank you," Honor smiled.

"Where's Seth?"

"He's here somewhere," Will looked around the crowded narthex. "There he is." Will waved his brother over, "Seth, over here."

Seth walked over to them. "Hey, Annie," he hugged her. "It's been a long time."

"It's good to see you," she hugged him back. "I have seats for you guys up front. I just need to check on Val, then I'll join you."

"You're not in the wedding?" Seth asked.

"Oh goodness, no. I hate the whole bridesmaid gig. Not that being one of the Bride Attendants is any better?"

"Wait, one of the them?" Will asked with a puzzled look on his face.

"Yeah, she has three. Like I told you before, Val is a complete Bridezilla. I can't wait until this is all over. I should go," She kissed Will on the cheek. "I'll see you in a bit." She smiled as she turned and walked down the hallway.

An usher walked them down the aisle to their seats. Honor sat between her father and uncle. Will noticed a few people looking at him and his brother. He felt a little uneasy. The rumors that had gone through Alexberg about the McFadden brother's feud still lingered in the minds of those who hadn't seen them in years as they stared and whispered among themselves.

"Maybe we should hold hands," Seth teased. He too had noticed the stares.

"They'll get over it," Will said as he smiled and nodded at the on lookers.

"Get over what?" Honor asked.

"Nothing, sweetheart," Will put his arm around her shoulder and kissed the top of her head.

Annie walked down the aisle. She excused herself pass Seth and took her seat next to Will.

She took a deep breath. "Remind me not to help with weddings again," she said as she turned to Will.

He smiled and took her hand. Honor leaned forward and smiled at Annie and her father. She was happy to see them together.

The wedding procession began walking down the aisle. Brock walked with the groom to the front, then turned and watched the rest of the wedding party as they walked down and took their places on stage.

The Bridal procession began and everyone stood and looked toward the back of the sanctuary. Valerie and her father appeared in the doorway.

~~~

The Reception was held at The Red Barn, a beautiful recreational center, just outside of town. The outside of the building's siding was made up of old weathered boards and painted red, to look like an old pole barn. Inside the barn it was a large room with a stage and a dance floor. White lights were strung loosely along the rafters, giving the room a soft glow. The wedding decorations consisted of purple and silver balloons and shimmery streamers placed perfectly around the room.

Will and Annie watched Valerie and her new husband dance on the dance floor. The wedding party and the other guests mingled and danced. Honor was on the dance floor with Seth. She looked over at her father and smiled. Will smiled back.

"She's an amazing girl," Annie said to him as she placed her hand on his.

"Yeah, she's something else."

Will stood up; he took her by the hand. "May I have this dance?" he asked her as he bowed like a gentlemen.

"I'd love to," she smiled as she stood.

He kissed the top of her hand and led her to the dance floor. He drew her close as they swayed to the music.

"I have a confession to make."

"Oh yeah?"

"I can't dance very well."

"I kind of noticed that the second time you stepped on my toes."

"Oh, I'm sorry."

"It's okay," she smiled. "To tell you the truth, I'm haven't danced this slow in a long time."

"Well, you're doing better than me."

"Honor and your brother seem to have it," Anne pointed out.

"She's a natural, just like her mother," he smiled.

"It's really nice to see you and Seth getting along."

"It's what my mom wanted, so we're working on it." He smiled as he watch his daughter dance with Seth.

"All right let's pick things up," the DJ announced as he turned up the music.

"Dad," Honor ran over to him. "Dance with me!" She grabbed his hand. "You too Annie, come on, this is my song!" she continued as she dragged them to an open spot on the floor and began dancing along with the beat of the music.

~~~

The reception was coming to an end. Will, Seth and Honor were sitting at their table, watching the drunken wedding party and the few guests that were still on the dance floor. Honor leaned on her father and yawned.

"I'd better get you home and into bed," he hugged her.

"I'm not tired," she yawned again.

"Yes, you are." Will looked around the room until his eyes met Annie's from across the room. She was sitting and talking with some of her family.

"I can take her home," Seth offered. "Besides you are still on a date. You can't go home this early."

"It's almost eleven-thirty."

"Yeah, well, you got a beautiful woman eyeing you from across the room. There's no way you are leaving the party this early." Seth stood up and put his suit jacket around Honors shoulders. "Come on, girl. Let's get you home."

"Are you sure?" Will asked. "I can take her home."

"Will, why do you think I drove separately from you? And why do you think I didn't enjoy the free bar?" Seth grinned. "I got you, Bro. Now go over there and spend some time with her. You deserve it."

"Thanks," Will said to his brother as he hugged Honor. "I'll see you at home."

"Goodnight, dad. Have fun."

"I will, sweetheart, love you." He kissed the top of her head.

"Love you too," Honor said as she and Seth walked together toward the door.

Will grabbed his jacket and flung it over his shoulder as he walked over to Annie.

"Hi," he smiled at her.

"Hi," she smiled back. She looked around behind him. "Did your brother take off?"

"Yeah, he took Honor home." Will gazed at her. "I was thinking about going for a walk. Want to come."

"Yes." She smiled as she took his hand, letting him lead her toward the door.

They walked slowly around to the side of the building onto a small sidewalk that led to the dimly lit gazebo. They were alone and could still hear the music faintly from inside.

Will set his suit jacket on the railing. "Can I have this dance?" Will grinned as he took her by the hand.

"Yes. Yes you can," she smiled.

Will twirled her around. He then drew her in close to him and wrapped his arms around her waist. She placed her hands on his shoulders. They swayed slowly to the music. She brushed her fingertips along the back of his head.

"I still can't get over your hair." She tickled the back of his neck.

"I can't get over how beautiful you are." Will smiled as he lean in and kissed her on the lips. She embraced him back as they kissed. Will slid his hands along behind her. His fingertips touching the bare skin on the small of her back. His breathing began to pace with the pounding of his heart as she too succumbed to their passion. He moved his lips from her mouth to her neck, kissing her below her ear. She tilted her head back as he glided his kisses to the front of her neck, just below her chin.

"Will," she gasped. "I thought we were going to..."

"I don't think I can wait anymore," he kissed her lips again as he wrapped his arms around her, drawing her body close to his. "Should we go to the truck?" he asked between breaths.

She nodded as they continued to embrace.

"We aren't getting very far," she giggled as he moved his lips back to her neck.

He grinned as he lifted her up into his arms to carry her to the truck. She wrapped her arms around his neck and locked lips with him.

"Annie!?!"

Annie and Will stop kissing and turned toward the man standing on the edge of the sidewalk.

"Eric!?!" Annie pulled away from Will's embrace. "What are you doing here?"

"My bus was delayed. What's going on? Who is this?"

Will set her feet on the ground and took a step back from Annie.

"Will...I," she hesitated. "I wanted to tell you..."

"I'm Eric. The fiancée of the woman you were just fondling," Eric interrupted as he stormed between them and poked Will aggressively in the chest with his finger.

Will grabbed his hand and pushed Eric way from him. "Back off, man," Will warned him.

Annie stepped in between the two men.

"Eric, I told you not to come here," she snapped at him.

"Annie, what is he talking about? Are you engaged to this guy?" Will asked her.

"She is engaged," Eric stepped in.

"Hey, I wasn't talking to you pal!" Will snapped at him.

"You cheated on me and I never said yes," Annie pushed Eric back. "Will, I needed some time to think and then you and I...Will, I didn't say yes."

"By the sound of it, you didn't say no either, did you?" Will inquired.

"Will, I was going to tell you - " she began.

"Annie, I thought we were going to talk about it," Eric interrupted. "That you just needed some space."

"Eric, I told you on the phone I didn't want to talk you."

"What about the baby?"

"The baby?" Will questioned. "What baby? Are you pregnant?" Will asked his eyes stared at her in disappointment.

"No, I'm not. I thought I was but I'm not," she tried to assure him. "Please, let me explain."

"Annie," Eric interrupted her. "You need to be talking to me. Not him."

Annie looked at Eric and then back at Will. She reached out to Will, "Will."

Will took a deep breath. "Okay," Will stepped back from her, shaking his head. "I should go. You two obviously have some talking to do."

"Will, please don't go," she pleaded with him.

"Yeah, I think you should," Eric glared at Will.

"Eric, please. Just stop," she snapped at him as she grabbed Will's hand. "Will, just let me explain."

"Annie don't!" he snapped at her. "Just let me have some time to think." He mocked her own words. He quickly grabbed his jacket and walked out into the parking lot toward his truck.

CHAPTER 15

Finn paced back and forth between the front door and the living room window; his whining and pacing woke Seth, who was asleep on the couch.

"Finn! Knock it off! Sit! Sit!"

He moaned and pulled his pillow over his head.

Finn stopped and looked at Seth as he peeked from beneath the pillow. Seth stared into the dog's eyes for a moment. "Now lay down," he commanded.

Finn just turned his head sideways at him.

"Sit! Flop, potz," Seth couldn't remember the German commands.

Finn nudged Seth's arm with his nose.

"Fine," Seth leaped up from the couch. "Okay, okay. I'll let you out." Finn ran to the door.

"Oh sure, he understands the word out, but doesn't know the word sit for anyone else to tell him what to do," Seth muttered as he walked to the front door and let Finn outside.

Finn raced out the door and darted straight for the willow tree.

"Finn! Here boy!" Seth shouted. "Damn it," Seth cursed as he walked out onto the porch and followed Finn to the tree.

Will was passed out against the tree, when Finn woke him up, licking his face rapidly.

"So either you had a good night or a really bad night," Seth teased his brother as he looked at the empty beer bottles scattered around the tree next to him.

"I don't want to talk about it. And can you please ... don't shout." Will pushed Finn back and curled up on the ground.

"So these are bottles of sorrow then?" he commented as he tapped one of the empty bottles with his foot.

Finn continued to nudge Will as he lay on the ground.

"Can you do me a favor and let Finn outside," Will moaned hiding his face in his arms.

"He is outside. You are outside."

"I am?" Will lifted his head and looked at Seth. Seth grinned back at him.

"Maybe a shower will clear things up for you," Seth put out his hand to help him up.

Will pushed his hand away and grunted as he grabbed the trunk of the tree. He stood up and staggered from beneath the shade of the long, tangled branches. He ungracefully tripped over the graveyard of bottles but managed to stay on his feet. Seth watched as his brother coward behind his hands when the sunlight hit his face.

"You don't look so good big brother. Are you sure you don't want to talk about it? Or don't you remember?"

"I remember, just fine. And No! I do not want to talk about it," Will warned as he stumbled toward his brother. Seth helped him steady himself.

"Come on, let's get you inside before the girl sees you."

Finn paced behind them as they walked back to the house.

~~~

Will let the hot water beat down on the back of his neck as he tilted his head back and forth and side to side. The heat felt good on his stiff neck. He placed his hand against the shower wall to steady himself as his eyes flooded with tears. He was overwhelmed with thoughts and the heartache. He didn't want to lose Annie. But she had lied to him, or didn't tell him everything she should have.

He gasped as he adjusted the temperature and stood under the water for a while before turning off the water. He grabbed the towel from the hook on the wall and wrapped it around his midsection as he stepped out of the shower. He wiped the condensation from the bathroom mirror. He looked into his reflection and into his bloodshot eyes. He took a deep breath as he opened up his bottle of Zoloft and took out one of the pills. He turn on the faucet as tossed it in his mouth and cupped his hands beneath the water and drank from his hands.

Will wandered into his bedroom. He pulled a pair of boxers from his dresser and put them on. He let the wet towel fall to the floor as he laid down on the bed. His head pounding from his hangover, he buried his forehead into his pillow and closed his eyes.

~~~

"Dad, get up!" Honor sat on the edge of his bed. "We are going to be late."

Will grumbled and pulled his pillow over his head.

"Dad," Honor shook his shoulders. "Get up. What's wrong with you?"

"Honor please I have a headache. Can you just leave me alone."

"But dad we have to go to church and we are going to be late. You hate being late."

"I'm not going, " Will grumbled from beneath the pillow. "Isn't Jo going?"

"She left early for Sunday school," Honor shook him again.

"Honor don't you think I'd be up and ready if I wanted to go to church," he snapped at her. "Now please just leave me alone."

Honor face turned red as she stormed out of her father's room and down the stairs. Seth was in the kitchen cutting vegetables at the counter when he heard her stomping down the stairs and sniffling as she ran out the front door. He set his knife down on the cutting board and walked towards the door.

"Honor?" he called out to her as he watched her flop down onto the porch steps. Seth walked outside and sat down next to her. She sniffled and tried to hide her face from him. He nudged her gently.

"Grown-ups suck," he said. "Now, I'm no expert but I heard that then people become adults, they forget what it's like to be a kid."

"He yelled at me," she sniffled. "He's never yells at me."

Seth put his arm around her. "Your dad had a rough night. He's just tired. I'm sure he didn't mean to yell."

"We were supposed to go to church. And Grandma left already."

"I can take you, if you want me to?" Seth offered. "And you could catch a ride back with Jo."

Honor wiped her face off with her sleeve and nodded her head.

"Come-on," he said as he hugged her. "I'll get my keys."

~~~

Seth gathered the empty bottles from beneath the tree and placed them in a wooden crate. He carried the crate to the old pole barn and set it down on the workbench.

Annie walked into the barn, caring a small cardboard box.

"Hey," she said as she approached Seth.

"Are you sure you should be here?" Seth asked as he looked at her.

"It's good to see you too, Seth," she replied. "So how much did he tell you?"

"He didn't tell me anything, that's between you and him. But whatever happened last night and the state that I found him in this morning tells me it wasn't good."

"Is he alright?"

"He's fine," he snapped at her. "I don't think you should be here."

"Look Seth, I just wanted to talk to him. He left before I could - "

"I just don't think he'd want to see you right now," he cut her off. "I'll let him know you stopped by."

"Seth, please. I know I screwed up. I just want to talk to him."

"No," Seth shook his head. "You know the last time you broke his heart, it nearly killed him. Now I don't know what happened last night, but I do know that he doesn't want to talk about it right now," he said. "Now I think you should go. He'll call you when he is ready."

Annie stood there for a moment as she felt Seth's glare burn through her.

"Here, these are for Honor. Be sure that she gets them," Annie handed the box to him. "Please just tell Will that I stopped by. And that I'm sorry."

Seth just nodded as he took the box. Annie walked towards the door, then looked back at him.

"You know, I thought you'd understand how it feels when someone can't forgive you. All you want is a chance to be heard," she said with tears in her eyes as she continued to walk out the door.

~~~

Will leaned against the kitchen counter, sipping on a cup of coffee when Seth walked into the back door.

"What's that?" Will asked.

"Some videos. Annie brought them over for Honor." He set the box down on the table.

Will looked out the window curiously. "Is she here?"

"No. I told her to go. That she shouldn't be here right now," Seth said as he walked over to the Crock-Pot that was sitting on the kitchen counter, and took the lid off.

Will stepped away from the window and looked at his brother, "You what?"

"Look, I know it's not any of my business, but what happened between you two last night?" he asked as he stirred the chili inside the pot.

Will took a deep breath, he set his coffee mug on the table as he sat down. "She has a fiancée I didn't know about. Anyway he showed up and I just didn't stick around to deal with it."

"So you came home and drank yourself to sleep?"

"It seemed like a good idea last night. But trust me I won't be doing that again," he said.

"You scared me, you know? This morning when I found you. It just reminded me of that night." Seth set the lid back onto the Crock-Pot.

"I just drank too much, that's all. I'm fine, really," Will assured him. "I'm not the guy I used to be."

"I hope not. Because we both know how that ends with that guy around," Seth said quietly as he walked out of the room.

CHAPTER 16

Seth pulled into the driveway, behind Will's truck and turned off the engine. His headlights automatically went out and the dark night overcame the property of his brother's home. He hadn't seen his brother since Rebecca's funeral. His jaw had mostly healed and he was ready, determined to mend things with his brother despite Will's wishes to stay away.

He stepped out of his blue Ford Mustang and walked up to the front door of his brother's house. He took a deep breath as he stood on the dark porch; the only lights were the dim streetlights, which blinked on and off. Seth knocked on the door and waited nervously. He knocked again and waited. Nothing. No answer. No movement within the house. He peeked in the nearby window. He couldn't see much through the undrawn blinds but he noticed the lamp next to his brother's La-Z-Boy was on.

He walked around to the back of the house and knocked on the rear door. Nothing. No answer. He sighed and walked back into the driveway when he heard something break from inside the house. Seth walked quickly back to the front of the house. He knocked on the door as he peeked the window once more. Will was now sitting in the lazy boy with a bottle in one hand and his pistol in his other. He stared blankly at the floor.

"WILL!" Seth yelled as he pounded on the door. "Will open the door!"

Will didn't move.

"WILL!" Seth shouted again and again. He continued to pound on the door and jiggle the door handle as he rammed his shoulder against the door, trying to break in the house.

Will got up from his chair and staggered to the door. He angrily pushed away the blinds with the muzzle of his pistol and glared out the window.

"Go away!" Will slurred.

"No. I'm not leaving until you let me in. Now open the damn door."

Will slammed his fist on the door as he fumbled with the door lock, his pistol still in hand. He whipped the door open. Seth slowly walked into the house and watched Will as he staggered back to his La-Z-Boy and sat down. He grabbed his bottle of Jack Daniels and took a long swig.

"Maybe you should take it easy with that," Seth walked cautiously toward his brother.

"Maybe you should go to hell," Will snapped at him as he wave his pistol around.

"Where's Honor?"

"Mom's. Not that it's any of your business," Will slurred as he continued to drink from his bottle.

"Will, why don't you give me that," Seth reached for the bottle.

"Why don't you get the hell out of my house!" Will jumped up from his chair and shoved Seth back as he pointed the pistol at his brother.

"Or what? You're going to shoot me now? " Seth took a step back with his hands out in front of him. "Put the gun down."

"It doesn't matter anymore," Will waved the pistol around. "We all have to go sometime. Becca is gone, Annie is gone, Dad is gone."

"What do you mean, Annie is gone? Will what did you do?" Seth fearfully asked.

"She's gone." Will flopped back into his chair, tapping the muzzle of his gun on head. "She gone and there is nothing left for me here." Will sat up straight and looked blankly at his pistol in his hands. "You should go. You can't be here," he said firmly.

"Will? What are you doing?"

"Yeah, you should go. There's no more to say. "

"Will, you are freaking me out. Why don't you just give me the gun?"

"You can have it after."

"After what? After you kill yourself?"

"It's better that way. There's nothing left." Will took another drink from the bottle as he continued to stare at the pistol.

"What about your daughter? Huh, you want Honor to grow up without her father? She needs you."

"She'll never know. Like I never existed."

"No she'll know that her father killed himself rather than thinking of her and what she needs. Come-on give me the gun."

"Just leave," Will glared at him. Seth shook his head.

"GO ON, GET OUT!" Will shouted as he raised his voice and the pistol at him.

Seth lunged for the pistol. A loud ban ringed in his ears as he wobbled backwards and onto the floor. The left side of his ribs burned from the freshly exposed meat of his side beneath his arm. He stared at his brother in shock as he lifts his shirt, discovering the bullet had only grazed his flesh and hit the doorframe behind him.

Will dropped to his knees when he saw the blood run down his brother's side. He set the pistol down onto the floor as he realized what he had done.

"Seth-" he reached out to his brother.

"No, don't," Seth shook his head at him. "You've done enough." He snapped at him as he picked himself up from the floor, grasping his side to control the bleeding.

"Seth I…" Will stumbled on his words.

"You know what? Life isn't over. You are still alive. You have a beautiful daughter," Seth walked toward the door. "But if you want to kill yourself, go right ahead. But if you don't you've got to get help man, cause that little miracle that Becca left you with is going to need her father at his best," Seth snapped at him. "Get it together," Seth finished as he walked out the door with his brother still kneeling on the floor.

<center>~~~</center>

Will was awakened by a knock on the front door. He had passed out on the floor where his brother had left him. Disoriented, he picked himself up off the floor and staggered to the door.

He opened the door. Brock stood outside, his face full of concern.

"What do you want?" Will asked letting Brock in as he turned and walked to his chair.

Brock closed the door behind him, "I got a call this morning from your mom. Said that Seth came home with a flesh wound to his side." Brock noticed the bullet still lodged the doorframe. He brushed his fingers over the hole then looked at Will. "I was hoping that it wouldn't come to this. After the hospital you made it clear…"

"It's not what you think, it was an accident. The gun just went off." Will put his head in his hands.

"Son, are you alright?"

"No," Will said impatiently. "I just had a rough night."

"So it was Jack Daniels that had something to do with your brother getting injured?" Brock picked up the empty bottle.

Will glared at Brock, "Seth shouldn't have been here. I told him to stay away."

"Will, your brother loves you and he cares about you."

"Yeah well he didn't care about me that night. If he did she wouldn't be gone."

Brock sat down on the couch. Will knew what was coming, a sermon of some sort. Something about how one should seek God and only God,

101

love and forgiveness of his brother. But all Will could think about is her his wife Becca, and that she was gone. Gone because God took her from him and now Annie left because God wanted him to be alone for the rest of his life.

Brock had already started talking but Will couldn't hear him. He sat there with a blank stare on his face. Brock's lips kept moving yet he heard nothing. He looked at floor and saw the butt of the gun sticking out from beneath the couch. He looked at the doorframe and focused on the bullet in the wood, that could have easily been inside his brother if the gun was an inch more to the right.

Thoughts flooded in Will's head as he questioned himself. What had he done? Where is Seth now? What did he tell them? Why was he here? Why was Brock here?

He could hear his voice but Brock's words seemed to smear together as he continued to go on and on. Then when Brock mentioned Honor, Will snapped out of his own thoughts.

"Honor?" Will interrupted him. "What about Honor? Is she okay?"

Brock looked at him with a puzzled look on his face. He had not a clue that Will wasn't really listening. "Honor is fine. I was just saying how God blessed you with the best gift of all. Your daughter."

Will nodded, "How can He bless me and curse me at the same time. It seems cruel to take Becca when I need her the most." Wills eyes start to swell with tears. "I don't know if I can do this on my own."

Brock picked up the Bible sitting on one of the side tables. He wiped off the dust and handed it to Will. "You're not on your own."

CHAPTER 17

The house was filled with the aroma of roasted tomatoes, chuck roast and sweet honey cornbread.

"Oh my," Jo took a deep breath of air through her nostrils. "Smells like your Uncle is making his famous chili and honey corn bread," She said as she smelled.

"Well whatever it is smell a lot better than anything dad had ever made," Honor laughed as she ran into the kitchen. Jo smiled as she went up the stairs and into her room.

In the kitchen, Seth had just pulled out a sheet of corn bread from the oven when he noticed her enter the room.

"Just in time girl," Seth smiled as he set the hot pan on the oven mitts on the table. "I need a taste tester." He grabbed a spoon from the drawer and scooped out a spoonful of chili and handed it to her. "It's hot, so be careful." Honor blew on it and slowly slurped the chili off the spoon.

"Mmm," she responded. "That's the best chili ever." She licked the spoon clean.

"Thank you," Seth smiled.

"When are we eating?" she asked as she poked her finger lightly at the corn bread.

"Soon," he said. "Want to help me finish getting the salad ready and set the table."

"Sure," Honor shrugged her shoulders. "Does the cornbread need to be tested?" She smiled at him.

"Well of course it does." Seth grinned as he cut a bite size piece from the corner of the pan and handed it to her.

~~~

Honor finished chopping the lettuce as Seth set out the rest of the food on the table. She grabbed the plates and bowls from the cabinet and set the table. She then took the silverware from the drawer and placed them alongside each setting.

"Is that it? Can we eat?" she asked eagerly.

"Yeah." He looked around the kitchen at the placement of everything. "Go on and tell you dad and Jo that dinner is ready."

Honor skipped out of the kitchen and up the stairs.

"Grandma," Honor spoke softly as she walked into Jo's bedroom. Jo was resting on her bed, her back toward the door. "Grandma, dinner is ready," she spoke a little louder.

Jo turned and looked over her shoulder, "Thank you dear. I'll be down."

Honor smiled and nodded as she turned back into the hallway. She walked into her father's room.

"Dad," she called out as she walked over to his neatly made bed. His room was tidy as it always was. She walked over to the window and saw him outside walking toward the barn. She skipped back into the hallway and down the stairs. Finn greeted her at the front door and followed her as she stepped outside and walked to the barn.

"Dad. Dinner's ready," she told him.

"Okay," he answered her. He was admiring the bench his brother had finished. "Did you see this?"

"He finished it the other day. Come on dinner's ready," she told him again.

"Yeah I'm coming." He turned toward her. "Hey, you're not mad at me about this morning are you?"

She shrugged her shoulders.

"I didn't mean to yell at you, I'm sorry."

"I know. Uncle Seth talked to me about it."

"He did?"

"Yeah he said you just had a long night and that you were just really tired. And that you didn't mean it."

"Is that all he said."

Honor nodded.

Will sighed and smiled in relief. "Come-on let's go eat."

~~~

Will sat down at the head of the table as the other three sat down around the table. Will held his hands out to Honor and his mother as they held theirs out to Seth. They bowed their heads.

"Heavenly Father. Thank you for all that you have given us and all you have done for us. Please bless this food we are about to receive and may it fill and nourish us. Keep, guide and protect us. In your name. Amen."

"Amen," Seth repeated as he began to dish out the chili into his bowl.

"Sethaniel, honey, this looks great. Thank you," Jo smiled as she too filled her bowl.

"Your welcome."

"I helped with the salad," Honor said as she passed the salad to her father.

"It looks wonderful honey," Will said.

"So how was the wedding? Honor told me that you danced all night must have been an amazing reception," Jo asked.

"It was okay," Seth answered as he looked up at his brother.

"William, you must have had a good time. I didn't hear you come in last night," Jo continued.

"Yeah Dad, what time did you come home?" Honor smiled at him.

"Huh I don't know, it was late." Will tried to avoid eye contact with her but found himself looking over at his brother who was staring right back at him.

"Who wants cornbread?" Seth asked as he tried to steer the conversation in another direction.

"Me," Honor answered him as she lifted her plate toward him. Seth placed a portion on her plate.

"So William, when are you going to bring Annie over? You know we should have her over for dinner sometime," Jo asked.

"I don't know mom. She is pretty busy." Will looked at his brother again.

"Wasn't she just helping out with the wedding? Now that it's over with she can't be that busy."

"She still has family in town. She'll be tied up for the next few days anyways. You know with family stuff," Seth added as he tried to help his brother avoid having to tell the truth.

"Dad, did she say anything to you last night about the videos?" Honor asked leaping into the conversation.

"Huh, yeah actually. They are in that box over there." He pointed at the box sitting on the floor in the corner of the room.

"What videos?" Jo asked.

"Annie had some videos of Mom. Dad, can we call Annie and see if she wants to come over and watch them with us?"

Will started to get frustrated. "She's busy with family stuff."

"But you can call her and find out when a good time is," Honor continued to push the subject.

"Honey, I'm sorry but I can't call her," Will said sternly.

"Why not?"

"I just can't," he said loudly.

"William!" Jo corrected him. "What has gotten into you? Why can't you call Annie?"

Will took a deep breath, "I can't call her because I don't want too, okay. We aren't seeing each other anymore and that's that."

Everyone just sat there for a moment in silence. Will looked at his brother again.

"But you are still friends, right?" Honor asked unmindfully.

"Excuse me," Will said as he stood up from the table and walked out of the kitchen.

CHAPTER 18

Will sat quietly in the pew as he stared at the cross on the wall behind the pulpit. Pastor Brock walked out from the back room. He was surprised to see someone sitting in, what he thought was, an empty sanctuary.

"William?" Brock approached him.

"Pastor Brock."

"Just Brock, please, only the elderly ladies address me that way. Pastor is just a job title."

Will nodded as he looked back up at the cross. Brock sat down next to him.

"Have you talked to Him lately?"

"Don't you mean prayed to Him? Yes, everyday. But I, I just feel like it's…I still don't know what I'm suppose to do."

"Suppose to do?" asked Brock.

"It's not that I have lost faith. It's just that I feel like I'm in this continuous circle of failure."

"What do you mean by failure?"

"No matter how hard I work, I just can't seem to get ahead. Losing my job, coming back here because I can't afford to support myself, let alone my own daughter." Will looked at Brock. "Finding out that Mom is dying of cancer and not wanting to fight it." Will took a breath and looked down. "I thought that I had a chance to be happy with someone and now I know that-that wasn't meant to be. Just like I'm stuck in this hole and can't get out and no matter how much I pray about it just seems like He gets farther and farther away."

"He's not getting farther away. Did you ever think that He is actually getting closer and closer to you?" Brock put his hand on his shoulder. "It seems that He's at work for you just like before. You losing your job, He has opened a door for you; time with your mother that you wouldn't have had otherwise if you didn't move back, Honor having this time with her grandmother and your brother and your renewed friendship. None of this would have happened if you were still working in the city. Now you all are stronger together to prepare for what's to come. As a family. God did this. He has brought you all together. He's closer than you think. You just have to look at the path He has laid out in front of you and not the obstacles, or boulders if you will, that are truly only pebbles in your way."

Will nodded.

"Do you want to tell me about what happened with you and Annie?"

Will looked at him with a puzzled look. "How do you know?"

"You and Annie have become close again. And you missed church this morning, only to show up hours later looking for answers."

"Is it that obvious?" Will asked.

"Well I'm not a mind reader. I only assume that she's the one you were talking about being happy with."

"I found out last night that she had … there's another guy in her life, or something. He showed up at the reception last night and I didn't stick around to hear the whole thing. I was just so hurt, I felt like I was so stupid to believe that I had a real chance to be happy with her. I just went home and … and drank myself to sleep under a tree." He looked at Brock, he saw the disappointment in his eyes. "I know that was stupid and believe me I'm not like I was twelve years ago. But I snapped at Honor this morning and I almost did it again this afternoon. So I just walked out of the house and ended up in here. I don't want to be that man I once was."

"I knew this young man once, he was a new father who had just lost his wife. He was already struggling with PTSD and medicated it all with a 12 pack and a bottle of whiskey. This man is not sitting in front of me right now. The man in front of me now has the determination to do what it takes to survive whatever life will throw in front of him. You're going to make mistakes, but you don't have to live in them. You being here now proves that you're not that man you fear of becoming."

"I just don't know how - "

"You don't have to. The only thing you have to do is trust in Him. He will shed light on what you need to do you. Have patience. He didn't give you the Holy Spirit for nothing. Let it guide you in times that you don't know what to do. And don't give into things that may seem to help temporarily."

Will nodded.

"Remember William, you're not alone," Brock handed him a bible from the pew. "Can I pray with you?" Brock asked.

Will nodded, "Yes."

Brock placed his hand on Will's shoulder once more as both men bowed their heads.

~ ~ ~

Seth filled a large five-gallon bucket with hot water from the showerhead in the bathroom. He left it to sit in the tub as he reached under the sink and pulled out a box of super washing soda. He poured about a cup and a half of the wash into the bucket. Then took one of Will's beer bottles from the night before and stirred the mixture with it, before placing it, along with the rest of the bottles into the bucket to soak.

He had just dried his hand when he looked out the window and saw Will's truck pulling up to the house.

Will had just reached the porch when his brother walked out of the front door.

"Hey," Seth said as he looked his brother in the eyes.

"Hey," Will said back.

"You good?" Seth asked as Will nodded at him. "Good. I think your girl is okay. But you should talk to mom. She doesn't need to stress over your mood swings."

"Yeah, I know. Where is she?" Will asked.

"In her room," Seth told him quietly.

"She's in there a lot."

Seth nodded. "Yeah, I know. Exactly why she needs you to go up there to tell her you are okay."

Will nodded and smiled at his brother. "When did you become the big brother?" he teased him.

Seth laughed, "Just get up there."

Will smiled as he opened the front door, then turn back toward his brother. "You know, I've been thinking. Maybe you should work with me."

"What do you mean work with you?"

"I think maybe we should be partners. You know building decks and remodeling. You could use that artistic ability of yours to come up with a logo for our company."

"You'd really want to share a company with me? Why?"

"Why not? It's not like you're busy. You could work as much as you want. Save up for your traveling with your photography and help me when you're in town. I could use some creative insight on projects and right now I don't really have anybody I can trust, except you."

"Ah yeah, I'll think about it," Seth smiled.

"Okay," Will smiled as he turned and walked into the house.

Will walked up the stairs and knocked on Jo's door. "Mom," he said as he walked into her room. "Mom."

"William." She opened her eyes and patted the bed beside her.

Will closed the door behind him then walked over to her bed and sat down next to her. "How are you feeling?" he asked her.

"Better now that you are here," She smiled. "Just tired. How are you?"

"I'm okay."

"Are you sure? Seth told me about Annie. About this morning," she said with a concerned tone in her voice.

"Yeah he could've left that part out."

"It explains why you've been so moody today."

"Yeah I'm sorry that I just took off like that. But I'm good now."

"Are you sure?"

"Yeah, I'm good. I had some time to think. Time to pray. I'll be alright," he assured her.

"That's good to hear," she smiled. She closed her eyes and sighed.

"Mom, how about you?" he asked as he took her hand.

"I'm fine. Some days are harder than others," she smiled. "I'm not dying just yet if that is what you are worried about. Just tired. Tomorrow is another day. And I'm just resting up for what God has in store for me tomorrow."

Jo patted his hand and smiled, "Have you talked to her yet?"

Will shook his head and took a deep breath, "She has a fiancé or something."

"Or something? Sounds like you really don't know."

"I don't. And the way it went last night she didn't seem sure herself."

"So call her."

"Mom, I'm not going to - "

"William, you are not going to know unless you talk to her. These last few weeks you have been on cloud nine about that girl. Don't get pulled down over something that is as easy as a misunderstanding. Think about it," she said sternly.

Will smiled and nodded, "I'll let you rest." He kissed her hand before letting her go.

"I love you William. You are a strong man. Just like your father. But you can be stubborn. Call her."

"I love you too, mom. And I'll think about. Get some rest," he added as he stood and walked out of her room.

Will walked back down stairs. Finn greeted him at the bottom of the steps. He scratched Finn behind the ears. Then he heard her voice. Becca's voice coming from the other room. Will quickly followed her voice into the den where he found his daughter with her eyes locked on the T.V. screen. He stood still as he saw Becca on the screen; the sound of her voice mesmerized him.

"She was beautiful," Honor said when she noticed her father enter the room without looking away from the T.V.

"She was," he agreed with her as he took a seat next to her on the edge of the couch.

Honor sighed as she watched her mother and Annie in the video. The two girls laughing as they lip sang to music in Annie's childhood bedroom, the joy of their youthfulness and their innocents captured on film. She looked at her father who also was taken away, his eyes focused on the video as he was taken back in time.

"Is it okay if I'm still friends with Annie? Even if you're not?" she asked quietly.

"It's not that we aren't friends. It's just complicated right now," he said as he kept his eyes on the T.V.

"But I can still be friends with her though, right?" She looked at him.

"Yeah, you can still be friends," Will assured her, looking back at her as he nudged her so he could sit comfortable on the couch.

"So you won't be mad if I wanted to talk to her."

"No baby, you can talk to her anytime you want." He put his arm around her and snuggled with her as they continued to watch the video.

CHAPTER 19

Honor sat in the tree with her book. A blue jay sat on the branch above her. The bird's tweeting drew her attention from reading. She watched the bird for a moment until it flew away. She lifted her eyes toward the names carved on the trunk.

She wedged her book between two branches then climbed down from the tree. She ran over to her father's truck. Finn had been lying on the porch and perked his head up when he saw her climb into the back of the pick up truck. She shuffled through her father's tools in his toolbox.

Finn ran to her as she jumped back down and stuffed one of Will's work knifes into her pocket.

"Hey, boy," she patted him on the back as he followed her back to the tree.

She pulled herself up onto the lowest branch and proceeded to climb up to the tree as Finn stood up on his hind feet with his front paws on the trunk of the tree.

Honor balanced herself, placing her feet on two separate branches. She pulled the knife from her pocket and began digging the blade into the trunk below her parents' name. She finished her 'H' and started on the 'O' when the blade slipped and sliced her left hand that she had against the tree to steady herself.

"Fudge nugget!" She dropped the knife on the ground, just missing the dog below. The blade stuck into the ground with the handle pointing straight up. "Sorry boy." She winced, looking down at him as she held her bleeding hand with the other. As she shifted her weight from one of the branches beneath her feet, the other snapped. She gasped as she fell to the ground landing on her left arm. She screamed.

Finn ran over to her nudging her with his nose and pawing at her shoulder to roll her over. "Stop it Finn! Don't touch me!" she screamed at him, as she cried bracing her arm. Finn whimpered and barked as he paced frantically from her and the front porch. "DAD!" she balled loudly. "DADDY!"

Seth sat at the kitchen table with his laptop, his focus on the new logo was shattered by a heavy scratching coming from the front door.

"Will! What's up with your dog?" he shouted loudly to his brother.

Will came running down the stairs, when he too heard the barking and scratching coming from outside. Will paused for a moment, then heard her scream.

"Honor?" He opened the door as Finn barked loudly once more then darted back to the willow tree. Will saw Honor on the ground "Honor!" he shouted as he sprinted towards the tree.

Seth followed Will outside. He too dashed across the yard to the tree.

"Honor!" Will cradled her in his lap. "Baby!"

"My arm daddy, it hurts so bad," she sobbed.

"She's bleeding bad," Seth said as he knelt down, pulled his shirt off and wrapped her left hand in it.

"Ahhh stop! Don't touch it!" she screamed at him, as the light pressure of Seth placing the shirt to her hand, increasing the pain through her arm.

"Sorry girl," Seth apologized.

"Come on, baby." Will gently picked her up. She wailed loudly as the pain surged through her arm.

"William!" Jo shouted from the porch as she ran toward them.

Honor gasped. "Daddy it hurts!" she cried out.

"I know, baby. I've got you," he said as dashed toward his truck.

"Here," Seth helped Will open the passenger's side door. "I got her." Seth took Honor from Will and helped her inside the truck as Will ran around to the drivers side.

"We'll be right behind you," Seth said as he shut Honor's door.

Honor continued to cry and gasp from the pain.

"Hold on honey, I'll get you to the hospital." Will started the engine and sped out of the driveway and down the road.

"Come on, Finn," Seth commanded the dog inside the house. Finn ran inside as Seth grabbed his keys then ran back outside to his van where Jo was waiting for him.

~~~

When Seth and Jo arrived at the hospital, Will was sitting in the waiting room.

"How is she?" Jo asked. "Where is she?"

"Well, she got eleven stitches in her hand and they think she broke her arm in two places. She's getting x-rays right now. Then they'll set her arm."

"Poor girl." Jo sat down next to Will.

"Well she's a tough girl. Did she say what she was doing with a knife?" Seth asked.

"She wanted to carve her name with ours in the tree. And when she cut her hand the branch gave out and down she went."

"You kids and that tree. I swear that it has seen more joy, heartache and pain over the years to last a lifetime," Jo huffed at them.

"Mr. McFadden?" the nurse asked as she entered the waiting room. "She's back from x-ray and they are ready to set her arm now."

Will, Seth and Jo followed the nurse down the hallway into the room where Honor was. She was calmer now and a little dazed from the pain medicine she had been given. Her eyes lit up when she saw her family enter.

"Hey baby girl," Will said as he walked over to her and kissed the top of her head.

"You gave us a good scare, honey," Jo smiled as she patted her foot.

"Alright," the doctor said as he entered the room. "You ready to get that arm back into place?" he asked as he approached her.

Honor nodded.

"Mom, maybe we should wait out here," Seth said. "It's a little crowded in here." He smiled at Honor as he guided Jo to the hallway.

"Okay, let's begin," the doctor said as he placed the x-rays of her arm onto the light box on the wall.

~~~

Will and Honor walked out into the waiting room. Honor's arm was in a black cast and rested in an arm sling.

"Black. Nice choice," Seth commented. "How are you feeling?"

"Okay," Honor said quietly, still groggy from the pain medication. "Dad can we go home now?"

"Yes, let's get you home. You need to rest."

"I'll ride with you two," Jo requested.

"I need to grab a few things at the store. I'll see you all at home," Seth said.

"Uncle Seth?"

"Yeah."

"Can you get me some gummy bears?"

"Yeah anything for you girl," Seth smiled at her. "I'll see you guys at home."

~~~

Seth pushed a shopping cart around the large hardware store. He found the outdoor lighting section and selected a couple boxes of the white outdoor Christmas lights and a package of solar pathway lights. He placed the items in the cart along with the hundred and fifty foot long extension cord and a pack of heavy-duty zip ties. He then continued to wander through the aisles until he found the snack aisle. He looked for the gummy bears that Honor had requested in the candy section. When he couldn't find them he picked out a box of Star Wars fruit snacks instead and tossed them into the cart.

"Seth," Valerie pushed her empty cart next to his. She looked at the fruit snacks in his cart. "You know, I would have taken you as a Scooby Doo fruit snack kinda guy."

"Hey Val," he laughed. "They're for Honor. She broke her arm this morning falling out of a tree."

"Oh my God. Is she okay?"

"Yeah, she'll be fine," Seth assured her. "I thought you'd be on your honeymoon by now."

"We'll be heading to Cancun in a couple of days. What about you? I thought you'd be on your next adventure by now."

"I'm moving back in with the family. I'm gonna be working with Will. Maybe save up some money and get my own place here in town."

"So you're finally settling down? What about your photography?"

"I wouldn't say that I'm settling down. I'll still be traveling around, just not living out of my van."

"Huh."

"What?"

"I just never pictured you in one place for long. Kinda takes the mystery out of you." She smiled. "All you need now is to find someone to share your life with, like Greg and me."

"You know your friend Alisha?"

"Yeah."

"She gave me her number at the reception. Said she is wanting me to call her sometime."

"Good for you Alisha is awesome, she'd be good for you. Make sure you call her."

"I will," Seth smiled.

"You know you should have your brother call Annie. She's leaving in a few days and I know that she is still waiting to hear from him."

"That's on her, she lied to him. If he wanted to talk to her he would have called her."

"I was hoping you'd talk to Will. She said she tried to explain that her so-called fiancé cheated on her and had broken up with him weeks before she even set foot into town. The creep just showed up at the wrong time and before she could tell Will about him."

"Yeah, well she should have told him well before the wedding and before he got his hopes up about them being together."

"Seth, she is devastated about not telling him. She doesn't want to hurt him. Can you please just talk to him and tell him to give her a chance to explain what happened?"

Seth sighed, "I'll see what I can do."

"Thank you," she hugged him. "I guess I'll see you around. I hope Honor feels better soon."

Seth just nodded, "Have a good trip." He smiled as he walked toward the checkout lane.

~~~

Will walked around the willow tree. He pulled the book down from where Honor had left it wedged between two branches. He looked down and found the knife sticking up in the ground. He sighed as he picked it up and looked up at the trunk.

He carefully climbed up the tree to the names carved in the trunk. He braced himself, avoiding the broken branch. He rubbed his fingers along the 'H' Honor had carved. He placed the blade of the knife where she had started the 'O' and began to finish what she started.

~~~

Seth stepped out of his van. He saw Will jump down from the tree. He looked curiously at his brother as he walked over to him.

"Didn't we have enough excitement for one day down here?" Seth teased him as Will brushed himself off. "How is she?" Seth asked.

"Fine. The pain meds kicked in. She is out like a light." Will put the knife in his pocket and pulled out his phone. He scrolled through his photos and showed his brother the photo of Honor's name added to the carved names on the trunk.

"You finished it for her," Seth smiled.

"Yeah. The last thing we need is for her to go up there one handed to try to finish it herself."

"She'd probably try it too," he laughed. "Hey send that pic to me I have an idea."

Will flipped through his phone and sent the photo to his brother.

"Good. Then maybe you can help me with something."

CHAPTER 20

Honor sat on her bed with her back against the wall and her left arm propped up on a mountain of pillows that she collected from almost every room in the house.

She opened all of the individual packages of the Star Wars fruit snacks using her good hand and her teeth. She dumped them all out on the bed in front of her and discarded the packaging on the floor. She sorted them by color, then by character, eating the disfigured ones as she made noises for each one.

"Ah, Han Solo," she picked up one of the fruit snacks. "So handsome, so strong, yet so alone," she talked to the snack. "That's why your name is Solo. And that is how you will die. Alone. Solo-o." She ate the fruit snack then picked up the Chewbacca and growled like Chewy. "Oh it's okay Chewy."

Will knocked on the door and peeked his head in the room.

"Hey," he said as he entered her room.

"Hey," she acknowledged him as she stuffed more fruit snacks in her mouth.

"How are you feeling?" he asked picking up the wrappers off of the floor.

"Fine, but this thing is so itchy and weird." She tried to itch between the cast and her arm. "And I'm bored. How long do I have to be in this stupid cast?"

"Four to eight weeks. And no one said that you had to sit up here by yourself."

"But my pillow mountain is up here. It feels better when I have it like this."

"You have an arm swing."

"It's not the same," Honor rolled her eyes and continued to stuff the fruit snacks in her mouth.

"Well, why don't you put it on and come help me with something."

"Help you with what? I'm not exactly helpful with one arm. I have limitations you know."

"Never stopped you before. Like yesterday when you were so determined to open that jar of pickles in the kitchen."

"Yeah well that was different, I needed pickles."

"Oh yeah, that's right food is your motivation," he teased her. "Come on, you need a little fresh air."

Honor sighed and looked at her father, "Outside?"

"Yes, outside that is where you can get fresh air and sunshine."

"Fine," Honor sighed again as she scooted to the edge of her bed. "Are you at least going to tell me what I'm helping you with."

"You'll see," Will said as he helped her put the arm swing over her shoulder and helped her adjust her arm into it comfortably. He kissed her on the head as they walked out of her room.

~~~

"Grandma," Honor said softly as she gently shook Jo's shoulder.

"Honor, honey what time is it?"

"Time to get up. We have a surprise for you," Honor smiled as she helped Jo sit up.

"Surprise? What kind of surprise?"

"You'll see. Come on it's outside."

"Okay. But first could you get me a glass of water from the bathroom? I need to take my pills," Jo asked handing her the empty glass from her nightstand.

Honor walked into the bathroom and filled the glass from the faucet. She then walk back to her grandmother and handed it to her. Jo portioned her pills from three different bottles.

"Grandma, can I ask you something?"

"Yes," Jo responded as she place the pills in her mouth and took a drink of the water.

"Are those really helping? I mean you're sleeping a lot lately. And it seems like I don't see you very much anymore."

"Yes, they're helping." Jo sat on the edge of her bed.

"Are you in pain?"

"Some days are good and some days are bad and that's why I sleep a lot."

"Are you scared? You know," Honor looked into Jo eyes, "Of dying?"

"Of course not. I'm afraid of leaving you and your father and your uncle Seth. But I'm not afraid of dying." Jo patted the bed next to her.

"I don't want you to die," Honor sat down next to her.

"Oh honey, I don't plan on doing that just yet. But believe me I'm not really dying. I may leave this world but I will live on in the house of the Lord. Just like your mother. She lives in your heart, as will I when Jesus calls me. And when it's your time and your father's time we will all be back together."

"What about uncle Seth?"

"Well you and I need to work on him about that. He hasn't given himself to the Lord. We can't force it on him, but we can show him by loving him like Jesus loves us."

"I always thought he did believe in Jesus. He goes to church."

"Just going to church doesn't make you a believer. Now I know he believes in the idea but I'm not so sure he has full faith in Him. I used to be the same way as your uncle Sethaniel. Before I was diagnosed. I used to go to church with your grandfather every once in awhile, sitting in the pews listening to the sermons. It wasn't until I was faced with death for myself that I realized there's so much more than just sitting in a pew once a week. Having a relationship with Jesus is the way to heaven."

Honor smiled. "That's what dad says. Oh, we better get down stairs they are waiting for us," Honor said.

"Yes, let's go see that surprise," Jo said as she and Honor walked out of the bedroom.

~~~

"Okay mom keep your eyes closed until we get there," Seth said as he and Honor guided her out onto the porch and into the yard.

"I am. Where are we going?" she asked as she turned her head over her shoulder.

"You'll see." Will walked behind her. He placed his hands over her eyes to keep her from looking too soon. "No peeking."

"Okay wait right there," Seth said as he let go of her hand. He ran over to the willow tree. "Okay, on the count of three. One, two, three."

Seth plugged in the string of lights as Will removed his hand from her eyes.

Jo gasped at the sight before her. The willow tree was decorated with tiny little lights that illuminated the branches like tiny little flames. Will's beer bottles hung from the branches like lanterns. Photos that Seth had taken throughout the past few weeks were encased in a hard, waterproof resin. They were hung and swayed gently like wind chimes, just above the bench, which was sitting next to the tree facing the pond.

"Is that?" Jo asked as she walked over to the bench.

"Yep, it's the bench dad built." Seth smiled. "I thought he'd want you to have it."

"It's beautiful," she said as she admired the pictures beneath the lacquer. "Oh, look at these old photos. So this is what you were doing in the barn. Sethaniel it's just beautiful. Thank you."

"Look Grandma, I have my own swing now," Honor said as she climbed into the swing that hung from one of the sturdy branches.

"I see that now I don't have to worry about you breaking your other arm," she laughed.

"Yeah, no more climbing trees for a while," Will added as he handed Honor a flat wrapped present. "Here we have something for you too."

Honor tore off the paper. She smiled when she revealed the framed photo that her father had taken of the tree trunk with her name added to other names carved in the tree.

"You finished it?" she smiled as she leaped out of the swing and hugged her father. "Thank you."

CHAPTER 21

Will walked into the dark room where Honor had fallen asleep watching another one of Annie's videos. He sat down next to her on the couch and gently took the remote from her hand. He was about to stop the video when she appeared on the screen. Honor had been watching the video taken at their wedding, Annie had interviewed all their friends about him and Becca and what their friendship meant to them. She then turned the camera on herself.

"Will and Becca, I just wanted to say that I love you both so much and that I wish you all the best. Becca I have known you since we were little and I know that you and Will are going to be so happy together in this new chapter you two are starting together as husband and wife. I love you like a sister, you're my best friend. Will I have known you for a long time as well and I know that you are the best man for my girl. You are strong, caring, loving and compassionate. Perfect for my Becca, so take care of her and continue to love her unconditionally like you have since we were kids I love you guys. Bye."

Will pause the video as she smiled on the last word she spoke.
"She is leaving tomorrow," Seth said as he walked into the room.
"I know."
"Are you at least going to call her and say goodbye."
"I don't know." Will looked at his brother. "I don't really know what to say."
"You could start by saying; 'Hello, I'm sorry for being a jerk,'" Seth said sarcastically.

Honor grinned slightly at her uncle's remark. She was pretending to be asleep when her father walked into the room and she eavesdropped as she laid still on the couch.

"I wasn't a jerk," Will defended himself.

"Well, you kind of were. She tried to reach out to apologize and wanted you to hear her side of the story. And all you've been doing is ignoring her and that's being a jerk."

"You're the one who sent her away."

"Yeah because you were being a jerk and the wounds were too fresh. I was just saving you from saying something you'd regret later. But she's leaving tomorrow. I talked to Val. And she said the Annie was telling the truth about that guy and that creep just showed up at the wrong place at the wrong time."

"Yeah, well she should have told me about it. She thought she was pregnant."

"But she's not. And from what Val told me, she broke up with this guy weeks before she came home."

"Yeah? Maybe I'll call."

"I hope you do, cuz I know you man. If you don't, you're going to be playing that what if game in your head until you run into her again. If you run into her and by that time it could be too late."

~~~

Jo sat in the new swing beneath the willow. She sipped on a cup of hot tea as she watched Seth and Honor, whom were sitting on the bench, discussing what to draw on her cast.

"Just surprise me," Honor smiled. "I trust you. Just nothing girly, like flowers or cute things."

Seth pulled the cap off of his silver sharpie. "How about a tree. I could leave room between the branches that way you could have people sign in those spaces."

"A tree would be pretty, on such a dark cast. Fitting too, considering," Jo added with a smile.

"Yes. Do it," Honor smiled as she opened her book.

Will walked out of the house and down to the tree.

"Well, it's all set. You start school on Monday," Will said to Honor from behind her.

Honor rolled her eyes and stuck out her tongue. Seth grinned at her response toward her father.

"Maybe you'll get stuck with Mr. Williamson," Seth teased.

"Who is that?"

"He's one of the strangest teachers in Junior High."

"Why?"

"Seth don't. She doesn't need to know about that."

"What she has the right to know who to look out for being the new student."

"I don't even think he's teaching anymore. He had to have been in his fifties when he taught us."

"No he wasn't that old. He had to have been in his thirties."

"You guys had Mr. Williamson? Now you have to tell me about him." Honor looked at her father.

"Seth had him for homeroom and geography. Didn't have homework from his classes most of the time cause the guy was always hungover or something."

"Do tell. I love stories," Honor said excitedly.

"Well it seemed like almost everyday he could walk in the classroom and kick his shoes off, put his feet up on his desk and curl up in his chair with a blanket and fall asleep. If we tried waking him or ask him what we should be doing that day, he'd throw pencils at the ceiling. Then scream at us that we were giving him a damn headache. He told us to do whatever until the end of the class."

"Wouldn't he have gotten fired, sleeping during his classes?" Honor asked.

"Oh he would have had I'd know about it. Sethaniel, why is this the first I'm hearing about this?" Jo added.

"Oh mom, you had to have know. Why do you think I liked his class?"

"Didn't any of the other teacher find out?" Jo continued to ask.

"No cause we'd keep a look out. If any other teacher came to the classroom we would wake him up. And he'd go on pretending he was teaching the whole time."

"Oh maybe that's why he didn't give you any homework because you guys stuck up for him," Will mentioned.

"Dad, who was your teacher."

"Well there were all of them. But I'd have to say my favorite teacher was Mr. Denny," Will said.

"The science teacher?" Seth disagreed. "He wasn't mine."

"Oh you didn't like him cuz you couldn't sleep in his class," Will teased his brother.

"Yeah he'd always find the heaviest book in the room and drop it on the table next to your head if he caught you sleeping."

"Well you shouldn't have fallen asleep. You could have learned a lot from him," Will added. "He coached your mom and Annie in basketball," he said to Honor.

"Mom played basketball?"

"Yeah and she was really good too," Will smiled. "Annie wasn't too bad herself."

"Speaking of," Seth nodded his head toward the driveway.

Will watched as Annie's car pulled up next to the house. Seth and Honor looked at each other then at Will. Will took a deep breath.

"I'll be right back," Will excused himself as he walked toward the house.

"I hope he doesn't get mad that I called her," Honor confessed as she watched Annie get out of her car.

Seth looked at her then at Jo, who smiled and shrugged her shoulders.

"Well he'll get over it," Seth said as he watch Will and Annie walked toward each other in the driveway.

"Hey," Annie greeted Will nervously as she leaned on the back of her car.

"Hi," he said, folding his arms in front of him sternly, as he stared at her.

Annie bit her bottom lip. "I am sorry. I should have told you about Eric. The truth is that I didn't know what I wanted when I came home. Eric and I had broken up after I caught him cheating on me. In a way I didn't care about it because I wasn't happy with him anyways. And when I suspected that I could be pregnant, he proposed. That's when I came home. I just told him that I had a lot of things to think about and that I had Val's wedding to worry about. But then I saw you. And I thought … I thought that it was a sign. A sign that you and I were meant to have a second chance. And I know that I hurt you, again."

She stepped toward him and placed her hands on his arms. Will continued to look her in the eyes silently with a strict look on his face, allowing her to talk.

"Please, Will, believe me when I say that I'm truly sorry and I hope someday that you can forgive me," she pleaded.

Will took a deep breath and looked over his shoulder. He noticed that his family had been watching them because they quickly looked away as soon as they saw him look toward the tree.

"Okay," he responded as he softened his face toward her.

"Okay what?" she asked with a confused look on her face.

"Okay. I forgive you." He unfolded his arms allowing her hands to fall into his.

"Just like that?" she asked, surprised by his response.

"Yeah, just like that." He finally grinned at her.

"So you're not mad?" she continued to question him.

He shook his head as continued to grin at her.

"Thank you," she smiled back. "So, What now?"

"I don't know." He shrugged his shoulders. He looked back over at his family, whom were watching. "But I do know that someone is dying to talk to you again."

"I suppose I should go a say hello." Annie smiled as she looked toward the tree at his family.

"Yeah," he smiled, gazed into her eyes and stepped closer to her keeping her from walking away. He grinned as he cupped his hands gently around her face and drew her lips to his.

"So are we back to taking it slow?" she asked through his kiss.

"How about we take it where we left off. But you know without the whole ex-boyfriend thing," he teased, kissing her once more.

CHAPTER 22

Spring had come to an end. Will worked hard throughout the summer and spent his weekends with Annie when she came to visit them. Seth took a few photography jobs and continued to work with his brother. Honor had finished the seventh grade at her new school and even met a new friend named Andrew who also enjoyed reading. And Jo published a new book and began taking art classes at a senior center in the next town over.

~~~

The sun had yet to rise and the dawn's light glowed lightly against the horizon. Jo had awakened early and was already dressed when she walked down stairs. Barefoot she walked into the kitchen and made a fresh pot of coffee. She took her time stirring a spoonful of sugar into her cup of hot coffee as she glanced out the window.

The steam rose from her cup as she stepped outside and breathed in deep the crisp cool air. She walked across the yard; the damp grass chilled her bare feet as she walked toward the willow tree.

She gently glided her fingertips along the smooth lacquered bench, admiring the photographs of her family and friends. The memories her son sealed within the bench her beloved husband built. She smiled as she sat down and watched as the breeze brushed through the long branch of the tree. She leaned back comfortably and watched as the sun rose from beyond the pond that rippled here and there from the fish kissing the surface from beneath the water.

~~~

Seth stumbled out of bed. He could smell the fresh coffee aroma the filled the house. He walked into the hallway as he pulled his t-shirt over his head. He glanced into his mother's room and saw that her bed was neatly made and her slippers lay on the floor.

He walked down the stairs and into the kitchen. He poured himself a cup of coffee as he glanced out the window. He saw his mother sitting beneath the willow. He took a sip of the warm coffee and set his cup onto the counter as he walked outside and across the yard.

"Mom?" he called out to her as he approached her from behind. "Morning mom."

She sat still on the bench, her hands in her lap and her head tilted toward her chest.

"Hey. You fall asleep out here?" he asked her as he got closer. "Mom?"

He watched her for a moment as he realized that her chest did not rise nor fall. Her coffee mug laid on it's side on the ground.

"Mom." He touched her wrist to check for a pulse. He felt nothing but her cool skin against his fingertips. Seth fell to his knee beside her as tears swelled into his eyes. He held her hand as he laid his head on her knee as he wept.

~~~

Will had just walked into the kitchen when Seth walked back into the house. He noticed his brother's face, the blank stare in his puffy eyes.

"Seth, what's wrong? Where's mom?" Will asked.

Seth shook his head as his eyes began to flood with tears again. "Better call Pastor Brock," he sniffled. "She's gone."

Will felt his face flush and his heart drop when he heard the words of, *She's gone*, fall from his brother's lips as if in slow motion, like a dream. Speechless, Will shook his head. "W-where?" he managed to ask.

"Where she wanted to be," Seth replied quietly as he moved from the doorway so his brother could see past him and toward the tree. Will took a deep breath. "I'm gonna make some calls," Seth said in a somber tone as he watched his brother hesitate for a moment before he walked out the door.

~~~

Annie walked out onto the porch behind Honor. Honor sat on the steps of the porch and stared at the willow tree. Finn sat next to her with his head on her lap as she stroked his ears. Her arm had healed. She had her cast removed several days before and she was still getting use to cast-less skin. She tried to focus on the weird sensation she felt on her skin with of every stroke against Finn's fur.

"Hey," Annie sighed, as she sat down next to her.

"Do you think she knew?" Honor asked. "Do you think she knew she was going to die today?"

Annie was unsure how to respond. "I don't know, honey."

"I think she did. She wanted to be in her favorite spot. She wanted to be beneath the willow," Honor said with confidence as she wiped a tear from her cheek. Annie wrapped her arm around Honor's shoulder and drew her close as they watched Will talking to one of the medics next to the ambulance beneath the tree.

Will shook the hands of the medics as they prepared to leave. Then Will, Seth and Pastor Brock waited under the tree until the ambulance drove down the driveway with Jo inside.

Annie stood to her feet and greeted Will when the men walked up to the house.

"Thank you for coming so quickly. It means a lot," he said to her as they hugged.

"You know I'll always be here for you. Both of you." She smiled at Honor.

Honor stood up and walked over to them. Will wrap his arms around her. He held her tightly as she buried her face into his chest.

"Hey, it's going to be okay. We talked about this day, remember?" he said softly. She nodded her head against his chest. He felt his shirt dampen as she sobbed.

Seth patted Honor on the back as he looked at his brother. "I'll get some coffee going."

Will nodded at him.

"I'll give you a hand," Annie offered as she smiled and placed her hand on Honor's shoulder. She then walked with Seth into the house.

"William," Brock shook his hand. "I'm going to go to the church and start making some arrangements. Please call me if there's anything else I can do for you and your family."

"Thank you. I call you when Seth and I get the obituary put together."

"Didn't she tell you?" Brock looked at him. "Your mother wrote it."

Will gave him a slight smile. "Well she is a great writer. I guess she should have the final words." He smiled at Honor then turned back to Brock. "You don't happen to a copy of it do you?"

"I'll email it to you, that way you can make changes if you need to."

"That would be fine. Thank you, again." Will shook his hand again.

"You are very welcome. And you," he turned to Honor "Take care of your father and your uncle for me. Call me if you need anything, okay?"

Honor smiled, "Okay."

They watched as Brock got into his jeep, and drove down the driveway. Will turned to Honor. "Come on. Let's go for a walk." He squeezed her and then released her.

They walked along the driveway quietly with Finn by their side. Honor stared at the ground as Will looked ahead. They walked through the tunnel of trees, the sunlight peeked through the branches creating spots of light on the gravel driveway.

"Do you think you go to heaven right away when die?" Honor asked her father.

"Yes, yes I do."

"So do you think Grandma is with mom now?"

"I know she is." Will said confidently as he put his arm around her. "They are probably up there, talking about us right now." He smiled at her. Honor looked up at her father and smiled back.

ABOUT THE AUTHOR

J.C. Hamm lives with her family in Iowa. She studied Art and Theater at Indian Hills Community College in Ottumwa, Iowa. She began her art career at a very early age and continues to draw and paint under her artist name, Hambo. She began writing poetry and short stories as a teenager and has a passion for film. Her first published Book "Because of Me" was originally written as a screenplay.

Made in the USA
Lexington, KY
08 June 2017